CW00456179

HOPE B[

The Moondreams House Romance Novels

Book Four

Ros Rendle

SAPERE
BOOKS

HOPE BLOOMS

Published by Sapere Books.

24 Trafalgar Road, Ilkley, LS29 8HH,
United Kingdom

saperebooks.com

ISBN: 978-0-85495-121-5

ACKNOWLEDGEMENTS

Thank you to Claire, who shared insights into the running of her flower shop, Manna Flowers, and who answered all my questions with patience.

Thank you also to the hero of Afghanistan — you know who you are — for answering questions about living with a residual limb and PTSD. That was particularly generous.

CHAPTER 1

Hope Everett had come home from the army at last, but she was still manoeuvring around the edges of it all. Tonight, she was at the thirtieth birthday party of someone she didn't know, which had been organised by her old friend Jacs. Hope watched from her table at the side of the marquee as Jacs and her partner, Malcolm, chatted with the guests. People began to crowd the dance area, and staff from the pub brought in trays of finger food.

When Jacs had suggested that Hope provide the flower arrangements for this party, she had jumped at the chance. She had been interested in floristry for a while but hadn't known how to start, so Jacs had taken her to an affordable flower warehouse to buy what she needed. Now, Hope was able to relax and admire her work, while observing the reactions of the guests. She'd arrived early so she could sit near the back where she could watch unobtrusively. It had been a long time since she'd attended a social function and having her work examined was nerve-wracking.

The first thing everyone noticed on entering the marquee was the scent, before remarking on the size and beauty of the arrangements. Hope smiled. It would be great to get another commission from this.

Hope had enjoyed everything about the process, even the barrage of questions from her mum, Dot. She thanked her stars that she'd had the opportunity to go to a series of floristry classes during her rehab. It had led to a City and Guilds Level 2 qualification, which she intended to take to the next level. She had managed to persuade the army to pay for it before her final discharge, although they had expected her to choose something with a more defined career path. In the end, they had agreed to let her take the classes if she also did a course on book-keeping. The floristry classes had been made up of young students straight from school, some older people, and several 'stay-at-home' spouses. They had all been exceedingly kind when they'd seen Hope's disability, and she'd loved the whole experience.

For this event, she had chosen yellow as the predominant colour for the arrangements, and the roses and lilies had the most pungent perfume. Alstroemeria, she had learned, was the correct name for the Peruvian lily. They added more colour and bulk but would last for quite a while. It had taken swear words and two re-starts to ensure the bouquets were successful, but she'd got there in the end and she'd learned much in the process. The shapes she had created in the low, wide vases had worked with comparatively few flowers.

Hope realised how few people she knew among the guests. She had been away for years, busy with training, postings and, more recently, hospital treatment, and she'd lost touch with her old crowd, apart from Jacs. Memories of her mum's dire warnings from when she'd signed up crept in, but she brushed them aside with determination.

The rhythm of the music from the DJ blasted through her, and she couldn't resist tapping her right foot. This level of volume was fine, as long as there was no sudden noise.

"You going to get up?" Jacs asked as she and Malcolm arrived at Hope's table. Jacs knew of her recent struggles, but she had sworn not to discuss them with anyone.

"Oh, I don't know." Hope shrank back, that familiar feeling of dread in her stomach. She could move in time to the beat, so long as she didn't overdo it, but it wouldn't be the same as when she used to dance with gusto. "Maybe later." The fear of looking staggeringly drunk when she'd hardly had a drop hung inside her head like the dusty cobweb it had become over the months of struggle.

She held up her wine glass. "A little more Dutch courage." She grinned, knowing it must look as brittle as it felt.

"We'll hold you to that, won't we?" Jacs turned and leaned into Malcolm.

There were few tables fully occupied as people mingled, helped themselves to food, or danced. As Jacs and Malcolm moved on, Hope's eyes settled on a man sitting alone on the other side of the marquee, nursing a half-empty pint glass. He seemed to become aware of her gaze upon him and looked across at her, raising his drink. A dazzling smile lit up his face, and Hope felt heat creep up her neck and into the roots of her blonde bobbed hair. She looked away to study the dancers.

After a few moments, a deep voice broke into her thoughts. "May I?"

Hope whipped her head round and she saw the man who had raised his glass to her. His hand was now on the back of the chair next to her. She took in his long, tapered fingers and brown arms. His nails were short and clean, she noticed with approval. He looked tall, but then, she was sitting, so it was hard to judge and even if she had been standing, at five foot five most people were taller than her anyway. He was still smiling, and Hope noticed his eyes were blue and twinkling. She took in his wavy dark hair and the hint of stubble on his strong chin. His nose was crooked, but it didn't detract from his charm. There must be a story there somewhere. A fight? A childhood accident?

She shrugged and nodded, not wanting to seem rude, though she didn't want to make small talk.

"I saw Jacs trying to persuade you onto the floor," the man said. "She was doing the same to me a while ago. So, you haven't got your dancing toes in gear yet either?"

"No, not yet," Hope replied coolly.

"My name's Dante. We haven't met before."

"I've been away a lot."

"I take it you're one of Jacs's friends?"

Hope nodded.

"Malcolm and I were at school together, but I've been away for a while too," Dante said. "Do you live and work locally?"

"Live. Not work."

Hope knew she was being unhelpful with her monosyllabic answers, and the conversation dried up. She took a gulp of wine but left a good measure in the bottom of her glass. She didn't want to be beholden to this guy if he offered to buy her a drink.

Then, exactly as she feared, he said, "I'll get us another," and bounded away. When he returned, he placed the two drinks on the table and she thanked him, before he raised his glass to her. "Cheers."

"I must find the ladies' room," said Hope. Leaving her drink, she managed to stand without too much awkwardness. The mortifying thought that he might think her tipsy if she wobbled, returned yet again.

Her long white trousers hid her leg, and surely no one would notice if she limped a little. She took her time leaving the marquee to find the ladies' loo in the pub.

At that moment, there was a loud crash, and a collective cry went up. Hope flung herself against the pole of the doorway and crouched with her head down, her hands covering her hair. Then she realised that someone had dropped a metal tray and shattered some glasses, nothing worse. She was shaking as she hauled herself up, her eyes darting around to see who had witnessed her reaction. She clung to the pole with clammy hands, her heart racing as the breath had left her lungs. Nobody was looking at her; they were all watching the unfortunate bar person who was scurrying around, picking up pieces of broken glass. Still, she stood motionless for a moment to regain her equilibrium, before heading into the pub. It had been a while since she'd had such a reaction, but her post-traumatic stress disorder was still there.

Hope tried to decide if anyone would miss her if she left and considered phoning for a taxi. Jacs might realise that she'd gone, but not for a while. She went to the noticeboard by the pub door, where small cards were pinned. Among those for painters and decorators, mobile hairdressers and, bizarrely, a company selling sunglasses for dogs called Doggles, she found a number to call.

While she waited for the call to connect, a larger card caught her attention:

WANTED
Florist for a small start-up business
Moondreams House, Waterthorpe.
Terrific opportunity. Call to discuss.

A telephone number accompanied the advert. Could she apply? It would be a bold move, considering her lack of experience. She could possibly blag her way through an interview, and Jacs would concoct a reference, she was sure. If she went for a casual look around, it would help. She hadn't been to Moondreams House since she was a child, when she and her school friends had built camps in the grounds from fallen branches and bracken.

CHAPTER 2

Hope intrigued Dante. He considered her as he sat in the marquee and awaited her return. He was attracted to her petite figure and neat haircut but there was something indefinable, too. She seemed vulnerable, somehow. Insecure. She had met his attempts at conversation with clipped answers and yet, having been aware of her for quite some time, sitting there alone at the table, he had thought she seemed relaxed, tapping her foot in time to the music. Knowing how he had screwed up his courage to come to this party, and how he had sat tensed, clutching his glass, he admired her confidence.

He'd sat for quite some time, debating with himself whether or not to approach her, and having plucked up the courage, the young woman seemed to have disappeared. He didn't think he'd said or done anything rude. There had hardly been time. Maybe she thought he was being pushy, buying her a drink like that. All his old insecurities began to return. The more he considered his current position the more he thought it was a mistake to have returned from France. At least there he'd had a good job, a social life, even a relationship of sorts. He pictured himself back there and thought about what he had left behind…

Dante sat at his desk and looked around the office. His colleagues were dressed as he was, in jeans and short-sleeved open-necked shirts. He loved the relaxed atmosphere. No one wore a suit, never mind a tie. It was so much more sensible when the sun burned hot in a clear blue sky.

Opening the email, he sighed and re-read it for possibly the tenth time.

"Where are you going for lunch?" Jean-Pierre called across the room, interrupting his thoughts. "Fancy that new bistro opposite the théatre?"

"Yes, why not?" Dante answered in French. He spoke the language with ease now and even found himself thinking in French. He looked at his watch. "I need to make a phone call to a new client out at Humières to fix up a visit, then shall we go? Say ten minutes?" Closing the email that had occupied his thoughts almost exclusively since its arrival, he picked up his phone.

Dante loved the two hours they could take each day for lunch. It was so much more sensible than grabbing a sandwich at his desk and he normally had the company of one or two friends. He was the only foreigner at the finance company, but they had all made it easy for him. They teased him about being English, but had soon realised he could give as good as he got. The friendly banter was part of the carefree mood.

The heat hit them as they left the air-conditioned building and the sun shone from a cloudless sky. Crossing the River Loire via the Pont Cessart, Dante looked up at the solid Château de Saumur with its four massive turrets. "You know it was an English king, Henri deux, who built that. Our Henri." He laughed.

"It's ours now, though," Jean-Pierre countered, "so we had the final laugh." He grinned across at Dante and fisted his shoulder. They managed to grab a table for two outside the bistro and ordered from the set menu. *Terrine de campagne avec poire* and *steak frites*. The local wine was good and cheap so they had a carafe of the red between them. The pâté was dark and rich with wild boar meat but the pears lightened it. The steaks, thin but perfectly heated to *saignant* so the juices still ran red and soaked into the thin fries, were perfect. Placing his fork over his knife in the French way to show he'd finished his meal, Dante sat back in his chair holding his wine glass but not drinking. The noises of the street faded. He considered the email, once again, gripped by indecision. In his work he acted with confidence, so how was it he was still placed in this position by a father he considered almost a stranger.

"You seem distracted," Jean-Pierre said.

Dante sighed. "I have a dilemma."

"Do you wish to tell me, my friend?"

"If I do, then you mustn't say anything to anyone just yet. I'm still undecided."

"Fair enough, but sometimes it helps to share."

"I've had an email from my father." He paused. "The thing is … he wants me to go back home, except it's not really home."

"You have been here for several years now and you have never talked of returning to England. I thought your home was here in France."

"So did I. My father can be very persuasive, though. He's not getting any younger."

"Do you have any brothers or sisters? Can they not help?"

"No, there's only me." As a youth he'd run away when his mother died, put himself through college, working all hours at rubbish jobs to afford it. She was the only one who had stuck up for him when his father had done nothing but belittle him, comparing him to his brilliant younger brother. He considered everything that had happened to be his father's fault — it was the old man's fault his mother had died early. His cantankerous ways had probably put too much strain on her heart. And now here he was, almost begging him to return home to take up the reins of the family business.

He took a gulp from his glass and leaned for the carafe to refill it, sharing what was left with his friend.

"Enough of that." He dismissed further conversation. "The day is too fair to spoil it. I thought I might drive out to Maison Ackerman after work. I have a yearning for some Crémant de Loire for Saturday night's gathering. Sparkling wine goes well with everything."

"Ah! Jean-Baptiste Ackerman, so much wisdom in one man."

Dante looked at him quizzically.

"He said, surely you have heard it, 'bubbles are fleeting, emotion is eternal.' Is there to be something eternal announced on Saturday night, perhaps?"

"No, indeed not. It's Marie's birthday and that is definitely all it is."

"I thought perhaps Marie was taming you at last."

"Marie is contemplating a job in Kenya, growing peas."

"What? I though you and she were set for the long haul."

"We considered it but…" Dante shrugged and drained his glass. "Come on. We better get back." Having successfully closed down that conversation, Dante pushed back his chair and went to pay the bill.

Sitting alone in the marquee, Dante sighed. Yes, he'd given up much in France to return home to England. As he waited, glancing at his watch several times, Dante decided that the young woman had stood him up. He realised he had given her his own name but he hadn't got hers. He considered going to the bar for another pint, but decided against it as he was driving. That was it, then. He might as well go, for he certainly wasn't about to get up on the dancefloor.

CHAPTER 3

Hope woke with a start. The nightmare was less frequent these days, but it still left her in a dark place. The medics had told her it would get easier over time. Now, as she lay in her narrow bed in her childhood bedroom, she slowly emerged from the suffocating terror, drenched in sweat. The sounds outside her window gradually penetrated — cars' tyres rumbling along the road, a child's high-pitched voice, birdsong. She focused on the sweet music of the blackbird as she grasped the duvet under her chin with whitened knuckles, and tried to visualise the creature perched amid the delicately coloured blossom of the almond tree. She breathed deeply, further calming her racing heart, as the counsellor had rehearsed with her so many times.

The muffled sounds of her mum, Dot, moving around in the kitchen were far away and steady, with no sudden crashes to shock her. Hope's body relaxed, and she thought back to when she had first joined the army.

She'd managed to withstand the protests from her mum. "Why ever do you want to do that?" Dot had demanded. "It could be dangerous." When that had failed to dissuade Hope, she'd said, "You'll lose touch with all your friends. It's no life for a girl." That final remark had made Hope more determined than ever. "I can't face sitting in an office all day, and university is absolutely not for me, Mum. I need to do something different. I want to travel. Explore new places. The army offers that."

It hadn't been like that at all in reality. The days had been repetitive, even boring at times, though peppered with intense activity and fear. Overall, she'd enjoyed her time in uniform, and the camaraderie in Afghanistan had been incredible. It had to be, to survive at all.

She had always been naturally determined. How had her dad described her on her fifth birthday? "A coiled little bundle of energy, our lass." That was it. The phrase had puzzled her at the time as she'd sprung around the room, excited by the day ahead. As a child, she had been resolute to swim faster and win more races, to dive from the higher board.

Aside from her career in the army, Hope had also had a lifelong affinity with flowers. Growing up, she had restocked the window boxes at home every spring using her pocket money, and as a teenager she had been tempted to get a sunflower tattoo.

When she had lain in a hospital bed years later, she'd read about the meaning of sunflowers: they symbolised devoted love, loyalty, and good health. Her work in the armed forces had demanded trust and loyalty in abundance, and she had proven herself capable of that, without needing a tattoo to remind her. However, she had had no time for devoted love. Instead, Hope had focused her energy on developing her ability to lead, her tolerance of others, and learning to live in dire circumstances. Then, during her second deployment to Afghanistan, the worst had happened, though she'd come out of it extremely lightly, considering. She looked down at where her left foot should be as she sat up and swung herself around.

Her injury had been caused by a roadside explosive that had killed two of her colleagues. Another had lost far more than she. He had had two limbs amputated and was still battling psychological trauma and an alcohol addiction. Hope had used the strategies taught to her during her cognitive behavioural therapy sessions and schooled herself to be grateful. What was done, was done. She had no major regrets, despite having to re-learn how to look after herself even at the most basic level. Showering and going to the loo had been the worst. What adult wants help with that? For a while, a very short while, she had considered her worth, before dismissing the notion. That early youthful energy had stood her in good stead. She would carve a different path now and she would find success and happiness another way.

Dot called up the stairs to let her know that breakfast was ready, jolting Hope back to the present.

"Coming!" she replied. As she sat on the edge of her bed, she pulled the liner over her residual limb before reaching for her prosthesis. Then, bending her knee, she inserted it into the socket before pulling the sleeve up over her thigh. She then reached for her trousers and left shoe. Shoes were one of the greater frustrations at the moment. She couldn't cope with heels of any height, nor could she wiggle her polymer toes into boots. Sandals were out of the question during winter, and when she did wear them, Hope had to consider the strap thickness for firm support. So here she was, with one pair of canvas deck shoes that had to suit all occasions. Perhaps she might eventually be able to afford a prosthesis that was more articulated.

It had taken months to get to this stage. During that time, she had been filled with fear, frustration and gut-wrenching rage, the intensity of which had frightened her. Then came exhaustion and finally acceptance, when she had begun to think about her future. Though Hope felt that her duty was to the army, the thought of being desk-bound was more than she could endure.

She was still strongly affected by sudden, loud noises and was over-zealous about routines and double-checking locks. Because she'd been diagnosed with post-traumatic stress disorder, she still had automatic access to support, should it be required.

When Hope had finally left the army, she had waited for the compensation to come through before she had considered her future in more detail. She didn't want to live with her mum and dad forever, though she knew how much they liked having her around. Shaking away the introspection, Hope negotiated the stairs with care, holding the banister and running her other hand down the wall. She arrived in the kitchen, where her mum turned and beamed at her.

"Morning darling," said Dot. "Sleep all right?"

This had become the customary greeting, and Hope smiled. "Yes thanks." She made no mention of the nightmare. "I'm starving. That smells good." She nodded towards the pan on the stove.

Dot put the plate in front of her and Hope picked up her cutlery, thankful that she could still feed herself. She took nothing for granted these days.

"Do you remember Colin — my friend Heather's son?" asked her mum. "She was telling me yesterday that he's going through a messy divorce."

Hope knew where this was going. "Oh dear," was all she could manage. She remembered Colin from the school youth club as an arrogant teen. Still, perhaps he had improved with age.

"Heather said that he's really lonely at the moment."

"Mum, don't go there." Hope changed the subject with practised deftness. "I'll have to get to grips with an automatic so I can drive again. Thank goodness it was my left foot that I lost. That was lucky."

"Well … yes, I suppose so."

Hope grinned. Lucky? Yes, she was lucky. She was still here to taste the bacon; see the sun shine in the clear blue sky; smell the flowers; go out with her friends again. So many things.

At that moment, the blackbird began to give voice to the summer morning again. What a sweet iconic sound it was. Hope breathed out, relaxing.

A memory flashed into Hope's mind. It was of sand, and heat, the smell of the tent fabric, the mosquito pod with her photos pegged to the inside, and basic washing facilities. She smiled stoically as she remembered her painted toenails, covered by beige socks and black leather boots. More memories came unbidden: the incredibly brave and determined women and their children whom she had met during her time as a Female Engagement Officer. Some of them had never left their compound and were surprised and wary to meet a white woman in army kit who could speak a smattering of Pashto. When out on patrol with other soldiers and her captain, Hope had set aside her weapons in order to enter the villages they came across. Leaving the men, who were not allowed to go in, she had approached the local women. In the small houses, Hope had even occasionally taken off her helmet, against regulations, and shaken out her hair. In the highly volatile Upper Gereshk Valley, communities were close knit, patriarchal, and often the men were sympathetic to the other side. It was extremely difficult for these women, who desperately wanted to make their voices heard, and were beginning to defy tradition. It was a culturally sensitive and dangerous issue.

The blackbird's song penetrated her thoughts. Perhaps these flashbacks would become less frequent with time. Now, she needed to find a new direction. Doing the flower arrangements for Jacs had taken her mind off her previous life. Today she would visit Moondreams House.

CHAPTER 4

It was unaccountably hot for so early in the summer as Hope climbed out from the taxi at Moondreams House. She turned and surveyed her surroundings. The place had certainly changed since her childhood. As she craned her neck, she saw evidence of a new roof and the paintwork was fresh. At the bottom of the steps leading up to the huge and heavy front door, there were discreet navy-blue boards with gold writing. She walked closer to see what they said.

One of the boards announced *eMotion School of Dance*. In smaller lettering underneath, it said, *Ballroom & Latin, for beginners and improvers*, before stating that lessons were available in small groups or privately in the magnificent ballroom. Hope didn't know there was a ballroom and her estimation of the place altered. This might not be the place for her after all. It sounded very posh. She grinned as the image of herself staggering around such a dancefloor came to mind.

Still with a grin, she read the next board which advertised *Tea and Sweet Dreams* and invited her in for homemade light lunches, barista coffee, and a range of teas with homemade cakes. There was also a children's playroom, where parents could watch their little ones while enjoying a restful chat. An A-frame stood nearby, directing her to the entrance. Hope decided to go and investigate.

Holding the handrail, she climbed the steps rather than using the ramp, which looked like the perfect 1:12 gradient and was an appropriate width for wheelchair access. Hope had become an expert in such things during her rehabilitation. The hall in which she found herself was enormous, with a huge marble fireplace on the far side. She thought it could do with a flower display to enhance its antique grandeur, instead of the gaping hole that looked blackened by past fires. A large mirror above the fireplace reflected the chandelier that hung from the high ceiling. The carpet was faded but looked old and expensive.

Another A-frame to the left indicated the teashop in the same gold lettering as outside. It was all very tasteful but also different from what she was used to, being more familiar with army canteens or High Street franchises. Hope summoned up the courage for which she was known, both in the army and at the hospital, and followed the enticing smell of coffee and cakes into the room. Again, there was a high ceiling and a large marble fireplace, but the floor was more modern, with wooden boards. Someone had laid the tables with pristine white cloths under glass tops, and deep crimson napkins that matched the ceiling-to-floor drapes. Each table had a menu card standing in a small wooden block in the centre. Hope imagined tiny posies of seasonal wildflowers next to them. It would be cheap and effective, and would suit the antiquated ambiance of the place. In autumn, there could be snowberries with leaves, and in winter, holly-berried greenery and feathery yew.

"Hello." The voice lifted Hope from her reverie. "Have you had enough time to decide what you'd like?"

Hope looked up and saw a woman who was about her own age. Her blonde hair was in a ponytail, and she wore minimal makeup. Her voice was soft and melodic.

"Breakfast tea, please, and perhaps a slice of cake?"

"Of course. I don't think you've been here before," said the woman. "I'm Natalie. I run this place." She looked around the room. "Would you like to come up to the counter to see what we have? Or perhaps I could tell you?"

Hope wondered if Natalie had sensed her reluctance to stand. She smiled. "I'm sure you can tempt me if you have anything chocolatey."

"I made a millionaire drizzle cake this morning, and there are some slices of Malteser cake left. We're quiet in here at this time of day, but later they'll both be gone in a flash when the dancers come in before their class." She laughed warmly.

"It better be the Malteser cake before it all disappears," Hope said.

"I recommend it. I've flavoured the frosting with white chocolate, but the cake is dark and delicious. The Maltesers will melt in your mouth."

"You're a good saleswoman," said Hope.

"We have a book swap and some magazines in the corner, if you want something to look at."

Hope thanked Natalie but didn't get up. At the moment, it was pleasant to sit at the table and look across the pristine lawn, with the flower beds and lake beyond.

When Natalie brought her tea, she nodded at the view and said, "It's beautiful, isn't it? I'm so lucky to work here. I took a risk with all this, but I'm so pleased I did. It's such a wonderful atmosphere here. Like an extended family. The gardener is a Frenchman, Gilles. He and his family live in the gatehouse."

"He keeps it beautifully."

"Indeed, he does. I'll fetch your cake."

When it arrived, it was huge and delicious-looking.

"Oh my!" Hope exclaimed.

"I'll leave you to enjoy it. If you want anything else, let me know."

Hope attacked her cake. She hadn't intended to stay, but after she had finished such a huge portion, the tightness in her tummy made her want to walk down to the lake. Anyway, it was such a glorious day, with bright sunshine and a crisp blue sky. She asked Natalie if it was all right to explore the grounds.

"Oh yes, do that," Natalie said. "It's so peaceful. I like to take off my shoes and walk barefoot on the grass. Gilles keeps it in such good condition; it's soft and fresh, and it feels so cool on a day like this."

Hope smiled but didn't respond. Fortunately, Natalie didn't seem to notice her awkwardness.

"You can hire a small boat on the lake in the summer months," she went on. "There are lifejackets. Or you can sit under the weeping willow tree. David, who owns Moondreams House, has had a bench put in there. It's really secluded if you want to read or sit quietly. Go and enjoy it, and I hope we see you again."

Hope ambled across the grass to look at the wide, well-tended flower border. The tall foxgloves blended well with the sweet-smelling, pink daphne. The fiery orange of an ornamental grass complemented the last of the aconites at the front of the border, reminiscent of a pretty cottage garden. There was evidence of flowers to come which would be equally strong scented and vibrant at the start of the next season. It was enchanting and appealed to her interest in floral arranging.

After wandering down to the lake, Hope looked across at the enormous weeping willow and decided to shelter from the sun for a while. The willow branches swept down to the ground, creating a cool, green cave. The wooden bench that encircled the trunk had an all-weather cushion, and Hope brushed stray leaves from it and sat, taking a deep breath, and leaning back. After the fear and tension of her previous life, her soul craved peace. Natalie's words echoed in her head — *I'm so lucky to work here. I took a risk with all this, but I'm so pleased I did. It's such a wonderful atmosphere here. Like an extended family.*

She closed her eyes, and images flurried through her mind. There was shimmering heat and mirages across the landscape. There were cold nights, the smell of local women's cooking, their long clothes flapping in the breeze. There were bones and blood and… Hope's eyes flew open and she listened carefully. Her hypervigilance would surely ease soon. In the hospital they had said it would. Breathing deeply, Hope practised the relaxation techniques she'd been taught.

She closed her eyes again and shut out everything but the rustling leaves and the distant birdsong. After a while, she thought she should find somebody to ask about the floristry opportunity.

"I'm sorry," said a deep voice. "I didn't realise anyone was here."

Hope's eyes shot open again, and she sat up, tensing. She looked around and was surprised to see who it was.

Dante! His blue eyes were filled with amusement. "Hello. I don't normally see anyone here, but it's a favourite spot of mine. I believe we've met before — you're the mysterious flower-arranger from the party."

"I don't know what you mean — I'm not mysterious in any way," Hope said curtly.

"You pulled off a vanishing act worthy of a magician's assistant." Dante grinned.

"Oh, yes, sorry about that," Hope conceded guiltily. "I'm going now, anyway. I have to see someone at the house." She tried to sound business-like but hesitated to stand while he was there.

Since he appeared to insist on standing and watching her, she forced herself to think about getting up, but as she stood and turned to pick up her small rucksack, the inevitable wobble let her down, and she reached for the back of the bench. Before she knew it, Dante was by her side, and he took her elbow to support her.

"Steady," he said. "Take more water with it next time." He laughed.

Hope glared. "Thank you," she said. "I'll remember that. Now, if you'll excuse me, I have to go."

"I'm walking towards the house," said Dante. "We could go together." He led the way and held the curtain of willow fronds to one side, so she had no need to duck and stagger awkwardly out of her hiding place. "Who are you going to see?"

"The owner," she said.

"Ah, David Troughton. I imagine he'll be around. He doesn't go far these days, although he's planning a long getaway for next year."

"Right."

"Yes, it's been a heavy haul getting on top of this place. He'd retired once already, and the house was a virtual ruin for a while. He used to acquire and sell antiques, but that was several years ago. Now, the various enterprises here keep him busy. They're all independent franchises, but he has an overall view of things. I think by next year he'll be on top of things enough for him to take a back seat."

Hope said nothing, but she wondered how Dante was involved with Moondreams House. They reached the front door.

"Shall I go and find David for you?" Dante asked.

"I can manage, thank you. I'm sure if I ask Natalie in the teashop, she'll help me."

"It's no trouble. I'll be back soon."

Hope watched his rapid retreat. He was very presumptuous, she thought, irritated. Then she wondered if he really was being high-handed, or simply being helpful.

Dante hurried up the stairs at the far side of the hall. The portraits seemed to watch him with dark, glaring eyes. This house was full of unhappy memories, and he wondered yet again why he had allowed himself to be persuaded to return. Had any of these people, who lived here before, had similar troubled histories? Surely not, yet none of them smiled at him. He arrived at the door to David's private apartment and knocked.

"Father, are you there?" He'd long ago refrained from calling him 'Dad'. "There's a young lady downstairs who would like to speak with you."

David emerged from his office room. "Mm? Sorry, I was in the middle of a spreadsheet."

Dante looked at the furrowed brow and took it personally, as he had done so many times before. "She asked specifically for you. I wouldn't have bothered you, otherwise."

"No bother, my boy." David sighed. "Don't be so quick to think I'm criticising. I'm distracted, that's all."

"Can you blame me?" Dante muttered. "Anyway, she's waiting downstairs in the hall."

"What does she want?"

Dante thought his father still sounded gruff, even though he'd mellowed over the last few years. Since Annie had set up her dance school in the ballroom and Natalie had started Tea and Sweet Dreams, David's interest in the house had regenerated. He was more approachable now, but Dante still shrank in his father's presence.

He shook his head and frowned. "She didn't say. But she did the flower arrangements for the party I went to the other night, so maybe she's interested in the advert. Shall I tell her you'll be down?"

"Yes, I'll be there. Give me five minutes." David retreated back into his apartment.

Dante hesitated, wondering whether to wait for his father and try to make conversation again. Then, as he heard the quiet tap of fingers on a keyboard, he sighed. He shouldn't have come back from France; he had been wrong to imagine that things might be different between him and his father after all these years. He decided to go back downstairs alone. He pulled his thoughts back to the young woman waiting downstairs as he returned along the corridor, ignoring the glowering portraits. She seemed a strange mix of strength and under-confidence, and he couldn't guess why. One moment she was prickly and defensive and the next ... well, the next she seemed vulnerable. Yes, that was the word. He'd thought the same the first time they'd met, at the party.

When he arrived back in the hall, Hope was leaning on the marble mantelpiece, one leg stretched behind her while she rested the other in front. Her short blonde hair hung forward, concealing her features. Her style was that of a tomboy, with her white T-shirt and linen wide-legged trousers. Tomboy she may be, but she was certainly attractive.

Dante cleared his throat. "My father will be down in a few minutes," he said.

Hope looked up. "Your father? Why didn't you say?"

"It didn't come up. I've only returned recently. I had to, really."

A question was written on her features, but Dante chose not to elaborate.

CHAPTER 5

Soon after Dante's return, there were more footsteps, and Hope turned to see an elderly man descending the stairs. He was smart in an old-fashioned way, wearing a tweed jacket with brown leather elbow patches over his white shirt, highly polished brogues, and a knitted tie. As he reached the bottom step, he stuck out his hand and Hope moved forward to take it.

"Good afternoon," said the man. "I'm David Troughton. I believe you're here to see me, Miss…?"

"I'm Hope. Hope Everett," Hope said, remembering to omit Lieutenant. That was a past life and not relevant anymore, but it still seemed strange after so many years. "Miss," she added with a nod and a swift glance at Dante. She lifted her chin.

"Well, Miss Everett, how may I help you?"

"I saw your advertisement for a start-up floristry business."

"I see. And where was it that you saw this advertisement?"

"In the pub."

"Really? The pub?" David looked across at his son with a slight frown, and Hope guessed that Dante had been responsible for advertising the job. "Perhaps we had better go to the study." David led the way to a dark wooden door to the left of the fireplace. On entering, he indicated a chair on the far side of the room, while he took the one opposite. There was another fireplace between them, and Hope saw that the brass fender and the ancient-looking tile surround were spotless.

Dante stood awkwardly, but after a moment he took the large office chair, which stood before an enormous oak desk, and slid it forward to join them.

"Do you have experience with floristry?" David rested his elbows on the arms of his chair and steepled his long, thin fingers.

Hope raised her chin. "I've completed courses in both floristry and business. I've also got practical experience. I recently provided the flower arrangements for a large party, and I got two more commissions from that event. Perhaps you would tell me a little more about what you have in mind? The advertisement was brief." And Hope didn't want to have to elaborate on her qualifications.

David looked at Dante. "My son will tell you. It was his idea. We discussed it, but I hadn't realised he had placed advertisements."

Dante cleared his throat. "I decided to place that ad. There's one in the *Evening Telegraph* as well." He glanced at David, then turned his attention to Hope. "We have a wooden barn in the grounds. It's near the entrance to the kitchen garden, which is a walled area not too far from the house, and there are pathways leading to it. It was the old potting shed and crying out for conversion. So I thought it might make a good floristry business. There could be space for designing and arranging flowers, of course, but it could also sell small gifts, because several people have asked after such a thing. That's what Natalie told me." He looked at David again. "There's a good space, two rooms. We could ensure one of them has internet access for office equipment. We'd undertake to fit the larger area with a workbench and shelving. We're still extending the house as a business to ensure we maintain its upkeep, so we're continuing to expand. You've seen the teashop, I understand, and Annie runs the dance school. This would be another such franchise."

"You're saying it would all be fitted out?" Hope asked. "Would I have any say in that? I'd like to see it, and then we could discuss finer business arrangements if it's suitable. We would need to agree monthly fees for the franchise and what the development period might be, and so on." Hope was pleased that she'd agreed to do the bookkeeping course. She could sound as if she knew what she was talking about, at least. Her Armed Forces Compensation Scheme money and pension, though small, would continue to help until this was up and running — if she got the job.

"You say you have business experience as well as floristry knowledge?" asked David.

"Yes, I have qualifications," Hope answered. She detailed her City and Guilds certificates. "I can show you, but I didn't bring them with me today. May we look at the premises?"

Dante leapt to his feet. "Yes, yes, that's the best idea." He turned to David. "Are you coming, Father?"

"I'll leave it to you. See me when you're done, both of you, and we'll take it from there," David said.

Dante was halfway to the door, so he didn't see Hope stagger slightly as she rose. She glanced at David, but he was brushing a non-existent piece of fluff from his knee as she left the room.

Dante led her outside to the premises: it was a small, silver-grey barn.

"It was re-clad about two years ago," said Dante. "It's larch, so it's already turned from its original golden colour, but it should last for more than fifty years."

The windows and door, painted moss-green, complemented the wood beautifully. The roof was steeply sloped, with two skylights. The tall wall of weathered stones behind the barn sheltered the kitchen garden, which Hope could see through the wrought iron gates. Dante took a huge key from his pocket.

"What has the building been used for previously?" Hope asked.

"Originally it was for the kitchen gardener and his assistants. Nowadays, the current gardener, Gilles, has a smaller shed on the other side of the house." Dante pulled open one of the double doors.

Hope gasped. The ceiling had church-like proportions, and huge wooden beams and trusses, pegged at the joints, supported it. The floor was made of golden wood planks, all in amazingly good condition. Light streamed in through the skylights, and at one of the gable ends there was a beautiful stained-glass window.

Greys and pale blues swirled together at the bottom, like smoke which curled and spiralled up between flowers. From the base also, were darker shades of greys and brown that looked like dead leaves and bracts but as they rose they became shot with pinks and peach colours until still higher up they were scarlet and orange fire fingers of petals and sepals, and curlicues of greenery towards translucent glass that emphasised the shapes nearest the azure, aquamarine, and indigo heavens. Hope stared at its extraordinary beauty.

"Stunning isn't it?" Dante's voice brought her back to the moment. "It even has a name in the house archives. *The Beauty of Imperfection*. It's Art Nouveau and quite valuable."

"The imperfection being the dead leaves and flowers at the bottom, rising and turning into those rich colours." Hope was awestruck.

"Yes." Dante stood looking in silence before clearing his throat. "It has rounded leading, rather than flat, and the bevelled glass pieces date it to pre-1920s. The previous generation covered it during the last war to protect it, but it's survived, and we've had it checked and renovated. Some of the lead cames needed their joints re-doing, apparently. It was fascinating to learn about the construction. It was the window which gave me the idea for the use of this place, actually. It's been standing empty for too long. It needs the presence of flowers again."

So, he isn't all imperiousness, Hope thought as she watched Dante's expressions change. *There is a poetic side to this man.*

Hope was desperate to work here. It would be bliss to open that door each morning and lose herself in flower-arranging. She just had to hope that she would be given a chance.

CHAPTER 6

Several days later, Hope was called to visit Moondreams House again.

"In all honesty, we're uncertain of your experience," said Dante.

"But we're willing to discuss things further," added David, glancing at his son.

They laid out the terms of the franchise. Three months of free access before recompense started wasn't uncommon, from Hope's learning. Sometimes an owner might demand a substantial amount up front, but the terms David and Dante were asking for sounded promising. After the initial period, royalties and the franchisor fee would kick in. They discussed the percentages for this and some other questions about Hope's certification, before David said, "Perhaps you would wait in the hall while we make a decision."

Hope took a seat in the hall. Neither man had mentioned other candidates, but she began to doubt that she had been successful. She stood and walked to the long casement windows, gazing across the flower beds to the grass, trees and lake. A dark-haired man was bent over among the delphiniums, a trowel in one hand. He righted himself, stretched his back, and with a free hand pushed his hair, greying at the temples, away from his face. That must be Gilles, the gardener whom Natalie and Dante had mentioned. As Hope watched, a lady in a flowery dress and flat sandals approached him with a mug in her hand. Gilles kissed her, and she smiled up at him as she handed him his drink.

Hope's heart wrenched as she observed the short cameo. She had never experienced love like that. The euphoria of being with one person, and feeling confident that the love she felt for that person was reciprocated, had so far eluded her. Or had she avoided it? It was the first time her heart had swooped at the thought of it. Hope blinked. It must be the clean freshness of the place, the beauty, so different to her previous life.

At that moment, the study door opened and Hope jumped.

"Please come in and sit down, Miss Everett," David said. When she was settled, he went on, "I'm going to be honest with you: my son is unconvinced by your experience."

Hope looked across at Dante, whose face was expressionless.

"However, I do like your enthusiasm, and clearly you have some knowledge of business," he said. "We all have to start somewhere. Tell me: what were you doing before? I should have asked earlier."

Hope hesitated. "I was a lieutenant in the army. I left. All was honourable, but it has no bearing on what I want to do now. Any references I provide will be related to this line of work."

"Yes, quite so. Still, it shows you have resolve and spirit, my dear," David said. "Right, Dante will tell you what we suggest."

"We will fit the room according to your requirements. We would need to do that anyway, for whoever took the place. We suggest a six-month probationary period, and you will provide flower arrangements for a function of our choosing during that time, as well as running a flower and gift shop. I shall collaborate with you on the accountancy side. We shall have joint responsibility during the probationary period. We will meet monthly, at least, and after five months we will review the situation and decide whether to continue with the arrangement.

After all, it's our expenditure and reputation we are putting on the line. How does that sound?"

"Perhaps you need to consider this offer," David said. "Would two days suffice?"

Hope took a deep breath. "I would be happy for Dante to review things with me on a monthly basis, but I wouldn't need his assistance with the daily running of the business." She needed to assert herself. "I know about flowers and the markets. I understand what people want and like — perhaps better than he?" She tried to soften her tone.

"I think you do, my dear," David said, allowing a chuckle to escape, which made Dante frown.

Hope realised she may have sounded too prickly. "If you are happy to trust me with the daily running of things, I believe we could make a successful venture which would benefit all of us. I don't need to think any further: I'd love to work here."

They shook hands on it, then arranged a date to discuss the outfitting of the barn.

After she left the study, Hope craved something to drink. She headed into Tea and Sweet Dreams, this time collapsing onto a squashy leather sofa against the wall. When Natalie approached, she had no idea what to ask for.

"You have the look of someone who needs something a little stronger than tea," said Natalie with a smile. "I can do wine, if it helps, or perhaps you'd be happy with a cuppa, especially if you're driving."

Hope began to relax and looked up at her. "We're going to be fellow franchisees here."

Natalie's face lit up. "Really? Oh, that's wonderful." She sat down and gave her a brief hug. "Welcome to the fold. What will you be doing?"

"Flowers and gifts, in the small barn near the kitchen garden."

"Perfect. I shall have to talk to you about some table flowers and an arrangement for in here — perhaps in the fireplace. Now, what can I get you? It's on the house — this is a celebration."

Hope grinned. "A cup of tea would be very welcome."

"May I join you? It's quiet this afternoon." As Natalie returned to her counter, she smiled at Hope over her shoulder. "The back room is empty right now because there's a birthday party for a three-year-old in an hour. Then it'll be positively manic, but a young lady named Ellie is coming in to help."

Hope sank back into the cushions.

Natalie carried over their drinks and two huge slices of delicious-looking chocolate sponge, which had tiny pink and white marshmallows embedded in the frosting. "Tell me all about what you're going to be doing in the barn," Natalie said as she poured the tea.

Hope outlined her plans for the business. "Do you get on all right with Mr Troughton the younger?" she asked. "He and I will be working quite closely on the financial side of things, at least for the first six months."

"Dante? Yes, he lived in France for several years and I don't think he was keen to come back, but David is getting older, so he needs to share the responsibilities of running the house. Dante always got on much better with his mother, apparently."

"When did Dante leave?" Hope was curious.

"I get the impression that he left as soon as he was able. He must have been quite young — apparently it wasn't long after his mother died. He told me that she always stuck up for him, and as I say, they were close. At some point in his childhood his mother was away for some time, but I'm not sure what happened. Dante seems to blame his father for his mother leaving, although she did come back." Natalie shrugged and smiled. "I shouldn't gossip too much about the owners, though. You might have a commission soon — my mum and her partner Rick are planning to get engaged, at last. They've talked about doing something here at Moondreams House — maybe even a dance in the ballroom — so I think they'd be interested in your floral arrangements."

"I'd love to meet them and chat about it."

"I'll let them know. I'd better get on, now. The three-year-olds will be descending before I know it. Congratulations again — I'm so pleased you're joining us."

Back at her parents' house, Hope sat at the kitchen table, telling her mum everything that had happened. "The only worrying thing is having to collaborate with Dante Troughton. He might be a little overbearing."

"He sounds a bit insecure to me," said Dot. "It's worth biting your tongue for those first few months. This does seem like a great opening, especially since you have limited experience. I can hear your enthusiasm." She continued chopping vegetables as she spoke. "You need to get out more. But I know things are tricky, and you don't like people knowing about your injury."

Hope sighed. "It's so hard sometimes, but I don't want people feeling sorry for me."

Dot moved on. "I saw my friend, Heather, today. She was coming out of the supermarket as I was going in. We had quite a chat."

Hope smiled. "You always do. Once you get going, there's no stopping the two of you."

"It's sad about Colin's divorce, but she thinks he's ready to start again. He can't just stay at home." Dot gave Hope a look full of meaning.

"I go out," Hope said defensively. "I went to Jacs's do."

"Yes, of course, love. It's time you did a bit more, though — perhaps try going out with different people."

Hope sighed, then heard the front door open.

"Your dad's home early," said Dot.

"I'm definitely not going out with Colin," said Hope as her dad walked in.

"Is that Colin who's Heather and Dave's son? Nice lad, from what I hear," he said. He crossed the kitchen and kissed his wife. "He's got a good, responsible job as well. Accountancy, wasn't it, Dot? Dave said he's just had a promotion."

Hope changed the subject. "I went to follow up about that position today, Dad. I think it's going to work out."

"What? The flower thing?"

Hope went through the whole thing again.

"Hmm, doesn't sound much of a career, love. Still, if it's what you want to do in the meantime, then go for it. It'll be a nice little hobby for you."

"It's not a hobby, Dad," Hope replied firmly. "It's running a business. In time, I'll be able to employ an assistant. I'll be using the book-keeping skills I learned on my re-training courses, and I shall build it up as I go along. I'll be going to evening classes to further my expertise as well, so I shan't have time to babysit Colin or anyone else."

"Don't be mortgaging your present for your future in the respect of friendships, that's all. You aren't young forever, and you can leave these things too late," Dot said.

"Maybe I'm not destined for the family thing with children, anymore. Perhaps I'm meant to be a businesswoman with a flourishing empire, and this is the start of that."

Dot tutted and Hope grinned.

"She's teasing, Mum," Dad said.

Maybe she was, but right at this moment, Hope wasn't sure.

CHAPTER 7

Dante stood awkwardly in his tiny office at the back of Moondreams House. Hope stood opposite him, waiting for him to begin proceedings.

Unsure how to start, he asked about her background. "You said you were in the army?" He avoided her eyes as he moved papers around. "What was your role?"

Hope sighed. "Look, let's get this out of the way. It's hardly relevant. I was a lieutenant. The last role I had was working as a Female Engagement Officer in Afghanistan."

Dante was impressed. "Wow! What did that involve?"

"Patrols, with Third Rifles infantry. Entering villages. Talking with the local women."

"And did you have to carry a full kit?"

"Of course. Forty kilograms, usually. It was dangerous." She shrugged. "If we're to work together, I suppose you need to know a little about my past, but, as I said, it's not relevant. What about you?"

"I've spent the last few years building profitable accounts for a finance company in France, so I know quite a bit that may be of use to you." He wanted to impress her, but he was worried about sounding arrogant. His insecurities resurfaced, from years of comparing himself to his younger brother who everyone thought cleverer and more accomplished than he.

Hope nodded. "Shall we get on?"

"Yes, of course. We'd better go out to the barn first, and you can detail some of the requirements for fitting it out."

"This is the exciting part." Hope grinned and followed him through a small back door. He was charmed by her smile and her eager anticipation. They made their way across the walled kitchen garden, where the gardener was pulling up weeds.

"Morning, Gilles." Dante smiled and Gilles waved. "This is Hope. She's going to be working in the barn, selling flowers and gifts."

"*Bonjour.* That's marvellous, and just the thing to enhance this place." Gilles gave a little salute to Hope. "Good day."

Dante strode through the gate and across to the barn. As he unlocked the door, the reassuring smell of the wood hit him. Once or twice upon his return he had come here and simply stood, breathing in the scents and the memories. As a boy, he had escaped here for hours at a time. The old gardener, Tom, had filled the trays with moist soil and allowed Dante to help. Together they had pricked seedlings, and Tom had shown him how to repot the tiny new plants. Dante could remember leaning against Tom's leg and feeling the rough fabric of his dark blue dungarees. Tom had often rested a hand on his shoulder or ruffled his hair. He couldn't recall experiencing that kind of closeness with his father.

"Right." Dante clapped his hands, taking refuge in briskness. "The back room." He indicated the door on the far side. "I'm assuming you need an office." He moved towards the door, and Hope followed.

"Wow! It's as big as the other room. I'll also need a quiet corner away from shoppers to arrange flowers. Is there a water supply?"

"If you look through there," said Dante, indicating another door on the far side, "there's a toilet and wash basin."

"Perhaps we could pipe water along the wall to that far corner for a large Belfast sink? I would need that for flower-arranging."

"The water pressure should be good enough for that. I'll get a plumber to look at it."

"And could I have a long workbench over there, too, at standing height? If I need to sit, I can have a stool on wheels. Are you paying for all this?"

"Yes, it'll be in the agreement. If you go and someone else comes, we'll need all that anyway."

"You mean if I fail the probationary period." Hope turned away from him.

"I didn't mean that. Maybe you will be the one who wants to move on."

She shrugged and looked around. "Unlikely," she said, before she moved back to the main room. She stopped where the light filtered through the stained glass, making her hair glow. "We will need shelves for things we're selling, and another bench over here for gift wrapping and tills, perhaps with cupboards for storage underneath."

Dante made notes on his pad. "Perhaps a central island for items here?" he suggested.

"Yes, that would encourage circulation. We need people to come in and wander around, browsing. That way we can pick up impulse buyers as well as people looking for something in particular. I'm not sure if we need a cold store. I think for now the back room has less direct sunlight, so it will be cool enough to preserve the flowers between their arrival here and me selling them."

"We'll address that if it becomes a problem."

"Great. Still, once this is a registered enterprise, I'll be able to get deliveries at least twice each week."

Dante hoped that she saw he was trying to understand what she needed. He so wanted to rise in her estimation.

CHAPTER 8

Four weeks later, Hope and Dante were sitting in his office again. The work on the barn was progressing quickly and the most important fixtures were in place.

"The main thrust of the business will be flowers. That's my area of expertise and training, after all," Hope said. "But I've been planning the gifts I'd sell, too. There are jams and pickles — things which have a long shelf life. I know of a lovely range of upmarket picnic baskets, and then there's the usual fancy stationery and lower-priced things. I want to attract all sorts of people, but I want to sell things that are not easily available elsewhere — the sort of things people want to see and touch rather than buy online. I've found some really unusual things. I've brought the catalogues in case you want to see them." She looked up at Dante. He sat back in his chair, playing with his pen and watching her. She wondered if he was bored. "You can check prices if you want. See if the markup is realistic. I've studied the people who tend to visit the gardens and tearoom here, so I was aiming at that market first. Then there is fine porcelain, like mugs, teacups and small jugs. I've had a meeting with Sophie Manthorpe — she's a ceramics designer — and she would be happy to have an outlet here for her range. They would be immensely popular with your clientele. I'd need to sell vases, of course."

She stopped to take a breath and became aware of the intensity of Dante's gaze.

"You've clearly thought a lot about it," he said, sitting upright. "You'll remember that my father and I spoke about asking you to plan and produce flowers for an event. As it happens, a couple from the dance school, Mick and Morag, are thinking of having a celebration here."

"Oh wonderful! Natalie also told me that her mum and her partner might also be planning an engagement party. And she would like flowers for the tables in Tea and Sweet Dreams on a regular basis, and an arrangement on the mantlepiece. We'll need to agree a price for Mick and Morag's party, and I need to speak to them, of course."

Hope saw the look of surprise sweep across Dante's face and she smiled sweetly at him, pleased to have taken the wind from his sails.

"They've already decided a date — the evening of Saturday the eighteenth of August."

"Not many weeks away, but it's perfectly doable." Hope was enjoying herself. She'd show him that she could play the boss as much as he could.

"I'll leave you to cost it, but perhaps you would share it all with me before the event," Dante said, then he moved on. "Now, marketing. We need to publicise the grand opening. Perhaps we can invite guests of some standing as well as asking the general public. I thought local dignitaries like the chair of the council and the local MP would give it gravitas."

"What about a local celebrity to ceremoniously cut the ribbon and open it?"

"Good idea. There's the Peterborough football team."

Hope gave him a quizzical look. "A footballer? Really? I was thinking of someone with more universal appeal. There's the Olympian, Freddie Baxter. He's very popular and does charity events."

"Wasn't there someone local who was in that dancing programme on TV? A Paralympian. He had a beautiful blonde professional dancer for a partner. She might even come with him. Hey, he was in Afghanistan, too. Lost part of a leg or something?"

"Joe Garratt."

"Do you know him?"

"Er, no. The army is a big place. We can come back to that." Hope hastily changed the subject. This was getting too close for comfort. "We ought to provide some light refreshments. I could speak to Natalie about that, too; we shall need to come to an agreement about costs."

"Just some finger food and maybe prosecco and juices would do."

They settled on a plan. "I'll pursue a local celebrity," Hope insisted. Dante was keen to make a short speech, which Hope accepted.

"What name are you planning for the business? We should have decided that ages ago. We need to get a sign made." Dante wrote a note to himself.

"I had a few ideas. Maybe 'Moon Blooms' because we're at Moondreams House. Or 'Full Bloom'. That sounds a bit dull to me, though."

"How about 'Heaven S-C-E-N-T'?" Dante spelled out the second word.

Hope grinned and said, "A little corny? I was also thinking of 'Blossoms and Bows', but I said it wrong to my mum the other day and it came out as 'Bosoms and Blows'."

They laughed together. "Hmm, maybe not," Dante said. "Your name would fit well with something. 'Beautiful Hope's Blooms'? That seems appropriate."

Heat crept into Hope's cheeks. She looked down at her notebook. "I think 'Hope's Blooms' would tell everybody what it's about. We'd need to decide on a font, although perhaps the sign-writers would suggest ideas. Then there's all the stuff to sort out for a website. I'll need a catchy domain name to stand out from the crowd."

"I know lots of people who can provide exactly what you'd like. I'll contact a few as soon as we're finished here, and perhaps I'll ask advice on the name and get back to you?"

After finalising their next steps, they stopped for the day. Hope was ready for a cup of hot chocolate, and she needed to see Natalie about the flowers for the teashop. She looked at her watch. There was time to do that before leaving.

After Dante had locked the door and pocketed the key, he said, "I'll get another set cut for you. This one lives in the key cupboard in the main kitchen." They walked side by side along the path towards the front of the house. Hope looked up at his tanned face and said, "I'll see you next week."

The magic of Moondreams House, the sense of belonging to an extended family which Natalie had spoken of all those weeks ago, was beginning to weave its spell around Hope. Here she was on the threshold of opening her own little emporium. Things were really looking up at last.

Hope watched as Dante strode around the side of the house. He turned before he rounded the corner, raised his arm in salute, and a smile lit his countenance with warmth. Hope wondered why he couldn't relax more when they were working together. Why did she feel like he seemed to be holding back a part of himself? She must remember to ask Natalie why his relationship with his father was so spikey. David seemed pleasant enough and by all accounts was kind, gallant, and even funny.

CHAPTER 9

A few weeks later, Hope sat at her parents' kitchen table, ordering stock from the catalogues she had acquired. Some suppliers offered a sample, and she was pleased with many of the things she had already received. Careful financial planning was essential. She was putting all of her resources into this enterprise, and so marketing and publicity would be vital to ensure it paid off. Her thoughts wandered. It was frustrating that Natalie could tell her nothing more of Dante's relationship with his father, but then, when she considered it, she decided it was none of her business and had no bearing on her progress with the preparations for the opening. She wasn't really that interested, was she? After all, she didn't want her own background exposed. She mentally shrugged him out of her mind and started to order more stock.

There were nights when she tossed turned, as ideas and worries surfaced alongside flashbacks from Afghanistan. One night, she awoke hot and shaking following her usual nightmare. After calming herself, she moved to the window, glancing down at the driveway. A couple of weeks before, she had decided that she would be better off with a large car, since it would make it easier to transport her flower arrangements. She had finally found an automatic that suited her perfectly, and she loved the deep red colour. As soon as she'd met with the website guy, she would order a set of magnetic panels to go on the doors, which would display her shop's logo. Sufficiently distracted from her bad dreams, Hope slid back into bed.

Hope and Natalie had arranged to meet Morag and Mick from the dance school to discuss their engagement party further. As Hope arrived at Moondreams House, she glanced around, but there was no sign of Dante. She tried to analyse why she would even give him a thought as she parked her new car. Although he could be a little irascible at times, there was no doubt he was exceedingly attractive. She shrugged the thought away. Her relationship with Dante was purely professional.

Morag and Mick sat at the table in the window, holding hands and leaning into each other. With her recent thoughts of Dante still fresh, Hope's breath caught in her throat. The couple had their heads together, a look of unreserved love on their faces. Would she really be happy never to experience a love like that?

Hope took a seat opposite the couple and they both welcomed her; then Natalie appeared from the other side of the room, carrying a large tray with drinks and a plate of small cakes. She smiled warmly. "Lovely to see you," she said. "I'm delighted that you've chosen Moondreams House for your celebration."

"We'll make it a special occasion for you," Hope added. "I gather you'd like flowers on a theme. Have you had ideas for that already?"

Morag looked at Mick and smiled shyly. "I don't know if it's possible," she said uncertainly, "but ... well, we wondered about something with a moon shape, because of the name for this place. Maybe in blue and gold?"

"Oh, that would be perfect," Hope said with enthusiasm. She took out her sketchpad from her bag and a small packet of colouring pencils. "Something like this? For the blue, we could use some flowers like those in the garden over there." She nodded at the delphiniums. "You see the different shades? They're at their best at the moment. I can add other flowers to fill. Then I can create a pale-yellow crescent in the centre, rather than a round blob. It would look more like the moon than the sun. There's jasmine — they are small flowers on a woody stem, but I could get them to bend nicely into the shape of a new moon." She showed Morag her sketches, then turned to Natalie. "Perhaps we could have a long table over there in front of the fireplace, and this would be the large arrangement in the centre. Any gifts or cards could go on there, too. Then we could have small arrangements in the centre of each of the tables and blue or yellow napkins to match."

"That sounds wonderful," said Morag. She looked at Mick for approval and he nodded enthusiastically, putting his arm around her.

Hope smiled and felt a twinge of yearning.

"We thought we'd ask guests to wear shades of blue, and we'd do the same," said Morag. "It would look nice on the photos, don't you think?"

"It would," Hope agreed, and Morag beamed at her. "I'll price it up and get back to you quickly, so that you can decide whether it's within your budget. If it's too expensive, I can think again and remodel."

Conversation moved on, with Natalie suggesting food and drink for the event.

As Hope drove home, her mind was buzzing. She needed to buy trays, vases and structural materials. She and Natalie had also come to an agreement regarding table decorations for the teashop, and she'd asked David if she could provide a regular arrangement in the fireplace of the hall. All rooms led off from there, and so the teashop customers would see it as they entered.

In only a few days, all was in place. Hope only needed to visit the nearest flower warehouse to source the blooms.

Her meeting with Dante to discuss the design for the signage and website had been productive. The name 'Hope's Blooms' sounded too mundane, so Hope finally said, "How about losing the apostrophe and the 's'? We could call it 'Hope Blooms'. It sounds optimistic." They agreed on the name, and a graphic designer produced a header for the website. It was a traditional flower border with sunflowers and a blue sky just peeping along the top. A large bumblebee sat on one of the blooms, just off centre. It was perfect. The business name ran through the flowers, but the colour ensured it stood out beautifully, and the sign maker agreed that the writing would be easy to reproduce.

CHAPTER 10

Having finalised the arrangements for Morag and Mick's party, Hope now had to share her costings with Dante. She watched in silent anticipation as he sat behind his desk, looking at her paperwork. He was attractive in an undefined way, with his sandy hair falling forwards, but his frown lines deepened as she observed him.

"Well, you're not going to be earning a living on this party," he said finally.

Hope stood her ground. "This is similar to a loss leader for long-standing members of the Moondreams House community. I received two commissions from the party I did for Jacs and Malcolm, where I could charge a full price, and that's what I hope to do here — get other work from it. A normal markup on each stem would be slightly more than I've got there, but five per cent on that type of flower isn't bad and, as you can see, it's a much higher percentage for labour. I'm charging appropriately for the flowers and only a little below the regular for labour, so it's not even a loss."

"I see." Dante paused. "You've given this some thought, and your figures do appear accurate."

"Perhaps you'd like to look at the price I'll be charging your father for a weekly arrangement in the hall," Hope went on. "If we're able to agree on that, I'd like to discuss the possibility of opening for a Christmas special, with lights and displays in several rooms."

Dante looked at her with one eyebrow raised. "We might save that for next time. I have another meeting after this one with my father." His mouth tightened, then he sighed and returned to the papers to look at her suggested price for the weekly arrangements in the fireplace.

They haggled a little over the cost. Hope only gave way a little, and finally they reached an agreement. Dante grinned and a dimple appeared beside his mouth.

"What?" Hope said.

"I won't mistake you for a soft touch again," said Dante. "I seem to have a hard-headed businesswoman on my hands. Still, it's early days, and you need to be getting commissions from outside."

She came straight back. "We need to get the website up and running. What's the latest on that?"

They discussed this for a while, and Dante phoned the man who had designed the website for Annie's business, the eMotion School of Dance. He also presented Hope with spare keys to the barn, to her delight.

By the time she and Dante had finished, Hope was hungry. She pulled on her coat and hurried to Tea and Sweet Dreams, thinking that a tuna and cheese melt would make a good lunch.

Natalie winked at her while she served a customer with coffee and cake. Hope went to sit at a table and when Natalie arrived, she gave her order.

"Mind if I join you? I haven't stopped all morning. Ellie should be here any minute. She's the daughter of a good friend of Annie's." At that moment, Ellie arrived to take over, so Natalie relayed the orders and sat down heavily. "We're really busy these days. I'm certainly not complaining, though. I may even be able to afford another part-time employee. How's it going with you?"

Hope gave a brief overview.

"That's so exciting. Guess what? Someone asked me if there was a gift shop, and I said it was coming very soon."

Hope grinned. "Wow! That's great news."

"How're you and Dante getting along?"

Hope shook her head and blew out her cheeks. "I don't know what to make of him. One minute he's fine, and the next it's as if he's trying to press the point that he's the boss."

"I think he's unsure of himself," said Natalie. "Apparently, he and his younger brother, Roy, didn't get on as boys. He was one of those genius types and always receiving praise, so maybe Dante grew up in his shadow. That's hard for an older sibling. I get the impression he was a sad little boy."

On the way home, Hope had plenty to contemplate. Dante had clearly had a difficult childhood. She wondered where his brother was now, and if they still spoke to each other.

The next day, Hope made her way to the wholesalers. As she drove, she noticed that the bulb fields on either side of the road had almost finished flowering, and the armies of pickers had moved around to other areas of the Fens for the vegetables. She thought it must be back-breaking work. A powerful tractor, with a covered wagon attached, appeared to be the hub for the workers, but they didn't seem to have a place to rest.

Hope finally arrived at the warehouse and made her way inside. It was a sensory overload. There were flowers from places such as Italy, Holland, and South Africa, mixed with dried blooms and twigs. All their perfumes mingled with a damp, mossy odour.

Hope saw lisianthus in purple and white — always a good staple for arrangers — and a variety of dill that would make a great yellow filler flower. She was having second thoughts about the delphiniums she had suggested when she'd met Morag and Mick. They could be tricky to maintain in full bloom if the temperature wasn't right. There was a large bucket full of purply-blue statice over to one side, which Hope thought could make a good filler for the sky part of her arrangements.

Spoiled for choice, she consulted the list she had made before leaving home. She would start with the trays and foam she would need, before pricing up the flowers. Hope's naturally generous inclination was sorely tested as she looked at the arrays of colours and types of blooms. It would be so easy to pick and mix too much. She must activate restraint and use the acquired sense of planning she had practised so often in her previous work.

Hope spent a good half an hour browsing before she approached a sales person. "Excuse me, do you have a supply of ribbons and sundries, only I don't see them here?"

"They're out there, Duck," said the woman with a strong Fen accent. "Don't want to risk them getting splashed and the warehouse isn't even so full today."

Hope must have looked puzzled. "It's Monday, me Duck. No auction yesterday, was there? No auction, no deliveries today."

Hope pulled a face. "Of course, sorry. Through there?" She pointed to the arched access to one side. She should have realised and come another day. Still, it was less busy, and they had what she needed, but she was learning all the time. She would remember that if she had to come here to source the flowers from here in the future.

Hopefully, her business registration would come through soon and she would be able to open accounts with the larger warehouses, which should be slightly cheaper. She could arrange deliveries twice a week with the Flying Dutchman and his lorry, and the Dutch wholesaler would even courier flowers to her if she needed something in a hurry.

Thinking of transport reminded Hope she would need to advertise for a man, or woman, with a van. She couldn't do deliveries of flowers ordered at the same time as minding the shop and making the displays.

Having decided on flowers, Hope had a look at what foliage was on offer. There were bunches of parvifolia, with small, dark green leaves. Not really what she wanted. She looked at the ruscus, but that was too expensive and the leaves were too large. Then she spotted the grey-green eucalyptus leaves. If she used them sparingly, they would be perfect for the arrangement she was planning. She then selected some yellow roses and a bunch of beautiful, cream carnations.

There were also the house flowers to consider. For the first arrangement, Hope had thought to do something showy, so she bought three large buds of white lilies which would have a deep red heart when open, and some smaller calla lilies. The arrangement would last well, because the hall of the house was cool and away from the sun. She could easily forage for the greenery, and by the time she had added all the filler flowers and foliage, it would look stunning and a good advertisement for her new business. She must be sure to put a card beside the arrangement, to direct people to the shop.

On the drive back to Moondreams House, Hope wondered what Dante would make of her purchases. She had bought well and within budget, so she hoped he would recognise that. Her mind strayed further, and she pictured his face framed by his sandy hair, his broad shoulders, and his long legs. A shiver passed through her body, but then she took a breath and shook him from her thoughts.

CHAPTER 11

Dante sat in his poky office. He had furnished the room in a hurry with items sitting in odd corners from around the house. He hadn't been fussy. The only thing of value was his laptop, which sat softly humming in the silence that dominated.

"You could make use of my study," David had said. "I often work in my apartment now."

"I'm fine in the back room." Dante didn't plan on staying long enough to make a more permanent base and, anyway, he felt his father's presence in the study. He couldn't possibly feel at ease there.

He thought about Hope. He had decided from the start that he would maintain a business-like approach and, generally, he had done that. Yet he found himself increasingly attracted to her confidence, her enthusiasm, and her energy. He had business competence but she was brimming with positivity, he thought as he rationed himself a thin smile. In addition, she seemed to know what she was doing. She had stood her ground and justified her accounts to him. He had to admit that she had a good head for business.

He was well aware what she thought of him, too. Aloof. Uptight. His customary under-confidence, never far from the surface, kicked in. He had far less experience of life than she. What had he done but run away from a tricky situation, when his mother died, and eventually join a business in a cosy corner of France? He'd only returned to Moondreams House after considerable pressure from his father.

Still, theirs was a business arrangement and he had deliberately maintained an emotional distance from Hope. Then came the moment he'd given Hope her own set of keys for the barn. Hope's expression, as she received them, was one of ecstatic delight which was charming to behold. He had to admit it had warmed his heart.

The phone on his desk rang. It was his father, requesting a meeting. Dante sighed. The house was large, certainly, but this seemed very impersonal.

Along the wide corridor, the portraits stared down at him along the length of the wall. He stopped briefly before one and peered at the tiny gold plaque set into the heavy gold frame. John Mortimer. The painting was dated 1711. He was famed for his Lincolnshire Longwool sheep, the proceeds upon which the house was built. Everything about this place was soaked in history. It must have so many stories to tell of past lives.

Dante knocked on the door to his father's apartment, entering when he heard David call "Come."

"Sit down, son," David said. "There's something I must discuss more fully with you. The time has come."

Dante moved to sit on one of the buttoned leather sofas and David sat opposite. It wasn't comfortable, so he sat forwards and clutched his knees.

"Relax. It's nothing dire." David sat back and crossed his long legs. "It's time to move forwards. You know, I'm so pleased you decided to come home."

Home? Hardly, Dante thought.

"I've missed you." There was a pause but Dante didn't fill the silence. "You've been here long enough to see what we're building here. I've paid for quite a few modernisations. We've discussed the viability and you've come up with some excellent ideas. The house is coming alive again, and so am I."

Still Dante said nothing so David cleared his throat and continued.

"You know that Edith and I are very good friends. She cannot replace your mother, my boy. She's completely different, but good for me, and I think I help her, too."

Dante tensed at the mention of his mother, especially by his father, the cause of so many unhappy memories. He had loved her so much. She had been his mainstay until the day she died.

"What do you want me to say, Father?"

"Oh, Dante. I suppose I'm looking for your blessing, but at the very least that you'll stay and take over the reins here, now you've had a chance to see it all. It needs a younger, fresher outlook. The house is ready and so am I. And I hope you are, too. Otherwise, we'll have to consider selling." He gave his son an uncompromising gaze from under his brows.

Dante looked at his hands on his knees and realised his knuckles were white. So, this was it. Decision time. It was a huge responsibility. People would rely on him. There was Gilles, the gardener, and Mrs M, the housekeeper, as well as the rest of the household staff. There was Natalie's teashop and Annie's dance school to think about too. Then there was Hope. He thought again of the expression on her face when he'd handed over the keys to the barn. He could not dash her dreams now. And he couldn't run away any longer.

"Fine," he said.

"This'll all be easy for you," David said, smiling. "You have the management skills. Moondreams House will continue to grow under your guidance. And you never know," he made a stab at levity, "you may even grow to love it here, as I do."

Dante wasn't so sure. "What will you do?" he asked.

"Edith and I have decided to go travelling — we would like to see a bit of the world together while we're still able to do so."

"When do you plan to leave?"

"In a few months. It is a huge relief knowing the house will be in safe hands. I'm happy to leave it to you now." He stood and as he did so he muttered, "I'm proud of you, son."

It was said quietly and David avoided eye contact as he pushed himself upright, so Dante was uncertain he'd heard correctly.

CHAPTER 12

Morag and Mick were very pleased with Hope's floral arrangements, and the whole evening passed in a flurry of prosecco and cake. Morag looked radiant, with her pale skin and auburn hair complementing the deep blue and white satin sheen of her dress. Mick was all smiles as he placed his arm around her and gazed into her eyes. Natalie provided a magnificent spread of food, and the ambience of Tea and Sweet Dreams lent a sense of grandeur to the occasion.

After the guests had departed, Morag said, "That was a dream indeed. Thank you so much for the beautiful evening." Mick came up behind and placed his arms gently around her.

"It's charming that he can't keep from touching her," Hope said to Natalie later. "They seem to love each other very much."

"Mm," Natalie replied. "My partner Stephen and I don't seem so close at the moment. We're on a break, as they say. I love him and he says he loves me, but we're both so busy. We've become too focused on our respective businesses, trying to build them up. I think that's what it is, anyway. We said we'd take some time away from each other and see what happens."

Hope didn't know what to say, so she touched Natalie's arm and said nothing.

It was the day of the grand opening of Hope Blooms, and the sky was grey. This was not what Hope had imagined.

"It'll be fine," Dot said as Hope nibbled her breakfast. "You've worked your socks off for this. I hope that man,

Dante, appreciates what you're doing. Dad and I are so proud of you."

"Thanks, Mum. I better get going." Hope took a slurp of tea and hurried out.

When she arrived at Moondreams House, she paused for a moment to take in her premises. The sign above the barn door was striking but tasteful. The words 'Hope Blooms' were easily discernible, despite some letters being replaced by flower heads, and the little bee that adorned the sunflower was perfect.

Hope opened the door. The shelves held unusual but beautiful gifts, and her large flower arrangements were stunning. Natalie had left delicate and delicious-looking finger food in the back room, where it was cool, and she and Ellie would come in to pass around the plates once all the guests had arrived. A tray of glasses and bottles of prosecco and juice stood ready on the counter by the door.

Hope took a deep breath and went to hang up her jacket and tuck her bag into her desk drawer. As she pushed it shut, she heard the barn door open.

From her office, Hope saw Dante standing in the centre of the room. He was gazing at the beautiful stained-glass window, and as sunlight began to filter through, he smiled.

Hope watched him silently and wondered. One moment he was arguing with his father and showed no signs of loving his position as son and heir of this extraordinary house. The next he displayed full appreciation of this magical space.

As soon as he realised Hope was there, he cleared his throat and marched across the room. His voice was brusque and business-like. "All's ready, then! Let's hope it's a success."

"Yes, let's," Hope responded, catching a whiff of delicately spiced aftershave.

Natalie arrived. "Hi there." She grinned at Hope and went to stand next to Dante. Linking her arm through his, she continued, "It looks great, doesn't it? Hope's worked so hard, and so have you."

As Natalie smiled up at him, Hope experienced a jolt in her stomach. Natalie and Dante had known each other for a while, of course. It was natural that they would be familiar with each other.

Just then, the two local celebrities, Freddie Baxter and Joe Garratt arrived together and interrupted her contemplation. After handshakes all around, Dante moved away to open some bottles.

Guests began to pour in and everyone mingled, glasses in hand. Natalie and Ellie passed around their trays of food. Hope watched Dante; he was the perfect host, passing a comment here and a smile there. It wasn't difficult to follow his progress, since he was a head taller than most.

The moment came for the official speeches. After Dante had spoken, Freddie and Joe took over. They clearly knew each other well, and although Hope guessed that they were slightly merry from the prosecco, their talk was entertaining. Then they invited Hope to stand between them and wished her well with the new venture. She caught a glimpse of her parents. Her dad had the biggest grin of all and he gave her a congratulatory thumbs up.

Several guests queued up to buy gifts and flowers, so Hope was kept busy at the till. Her face ached from smiling so much, but inside she was glowing.

"Congratulations, Hope," said Dante as he drained his glass.

Natalie came across with a pile of plates balanced on a tray. "That went really well. Those two celebs were a smart choice."

"Here, let me take those for you," Dante said, seizing the tray.

"Thanks. I'll gather up another lot."

"I'll help too. Hang on while I sort out the till," Hope said.

Her residual limb was aching. She hadn't stood for so long in ages, but she was happy. The sales had been excellent, and people had taken her business cards.

Not even Dante's cautious parting words could dampen her spirit. "The following days will let us know if this is a success," he said. "Let's see how it goes."

CHAPTER 13

Hope and Natalie wandered down to the lake. They had both been busy and were now taking a break. Hope was keeping an eye on her barn in case anyone headed in that direction. That morning she had sold a high-end picnic basket as a wedding gift, as well as flowers and a vase. Her website was beginning to attract attention, and she'd been putting together birthday bouquets and one funeral wreath. The sun glinting on the lake was calming, the breeze wafted the reeds and the birdsong was peaceful.

"I can't say the business is sustaining me yet, but it's showing signs of promise," she said.

Natalie took off her sandals. "I love the feel of the grass between my toes when I've been on my feet all morning," she said.

Hope said nothing. She'd like to have taken off her shoe too, but Natalie knew nothing of her disability. No one at Moondreams House did. They walked in silence for several moments.

"Your opening night was fabulous," Natalie said. "The flowers in that big vase opposite the door were stunning. You're so skilled. Loads of people said so."

"It's a shame Dante wasn't as enthusiastic as you. He just said that we'd have to see whether the opening night has any effect on sales."

Natalie laughed gently. "Typical. He's never lavish with his praise, but he did say how lovely the room looked. And he sounded positive when he was talking about the website."

"Why couldn't he say that to me?" Hope burst out. "I honestly think he's not keen on me and thinks I'm going to make a hash of it all."

"I don't think that's it — probably quite the opposite," Natalie reassured her. "He's not confident, you know. Don't forget, I've known him for longer. He hides behind brusqueness."

"Right." Hope wasn't convinced.

"I wanted to tell you about something he said, the other night. Oh, hang on, I think you might have a customer." Natalie nodded at the path to the barn.

"I'd better go," Hope said. As she crossed the grass, she wondered what Natalie had been going to say.

"Come in for a drink after work!" Natalie called after her, and Hope waved and blew her a kiss.

After closing her shop, Hope entered the tearoom. It was late, and all but one of the customers had left. Ellie was wiping down the counter, and Natalie was sitting by the window with the remaining lady.

"Come and join us," she said as Hope entered. "Let me get you a glass of wine. You look like you could do with it. This is my mum, by the way, Maggie."

Hope pulled over another chair and sat down as Natalie handed her a glass. She took a sip. "Thank you. This is delicious." The Pinot Grigio was cool and crisp, but not too dry.

"So, you're the lass who's started up a flower business in the barn," Maggie said. "Just the person I need to talk to. My fiancé Rick and I would like to have a grand party in the ballroom to celebrate our engagement. Natalie's doing the food, aren't you darling? And we'll definitely need flowers."

Hope smiled. "I'd love to do that," she said. "You'll have to let me know about colours and styles. When is it to be?"

Maggie named the date, and Hope retrieved her phone and added it to her calendar.

"I must be off. Rick and I are going to the cinema tonight," said Maggie. "I'll come by the barn and speak to you as soon as possible. Or is it best to make an appointment?"

"Call in when you're ready and I can show you some designs," Hope said.

Natalie stood. "I'll be back in a minute. I'll just see Mum out and secure the door behind her." She smiled and winked at Hope. "There's something I must tell you."

When she came back, Hope tilted her head to one side. "You can't leave me hanging like that! What is it you have to tell me?" she asked.

"Okay." Natalie paused. "Dante and I went out for a drink the other night…"

"What? You had a date?" Hope was a little unsettled by that revelation. "Wow. Right."

Natalie didn't seem to notice as she rushed on. "He said David is thinking of retiring."

"Oh, goodness!" Hope said. "What will that mean for us? I'm only just starting out, and the business you have here is so magnificent. And then there's Annie's dance school…"

"Woah! It's not all doom and gloom. Dante says he'll have to take over. To be honest, I believe he thinks that would be easier all round. You know he doesn't get on with his father and if David goes, well, Dante will be able to do things his own way."

Hope grimaced.

"It could be the making of us all," insisted Natalie. "David has done a wonderful job, but he's tired and needs a break. This will be the second time he's retired. He used to be an antiques dealer, that's how he managed to acquire this property and fill it with so many beautiful things. He was really successful, apparently. The house began to fall into disrepair after his wife died, but then Annie came along and persuaded him to let her use the ballroom. David met Edith at one of Annie's dance classes, and now they're both ready to take a break and travel."

"When are they going?" Hope asked.

"Not sure exactly but in a month or two."

"That soon?" Hope mulled it over. She didn't see much of David, but he was kind and definitely on her side. With Dante, she was unsure. She took a gulp of her wine and then quickly drained her glass.

"Do you want another? Sorry if this is a bombshell, but I do think it'll be okay."

"I better not."

"Coffee then," said Natalie, walking over to the coffee machine.

After a pause, Hope said, "So, you went on a date with Dante." She smiled and tried to sound nonchalant.

"Sort of." The hissing of the machine meant that Natalie had to raise her voice to answer.

"I know you said that you and Stephen were on a break, but...?"

"I'm not sure if it was a real date. Dante and I are friends." Natalie shrugged. "He's lonely, I think."

Hope stared out of the window as she waited for Natalie to return with the coffees. Dante didn't seem to have any great love for the house, apart from perhaps her flower barn. He certainly had no fondness for his father. She just had to hope that he would look after the house sufficiently, so that her business had a chance to flourish.

CHAPTER 14

"There's another event." Dante played with his pen as he spoke. He and Hope were sitting in his office. "It will be in the ballroom, with dinner in the hall. And it will be significantly bigger than the one you did for Mick and Morag at Natalie's teashop."

"Yes, I already spoke to Natalie's mum, Maggie, about it." Hope paused. "That last one was a success, and I got a couple of commissions for large arrangements from it."

"The figures show that you *are* turning a *small* profit."

"There you are, then. It's early days, and to be turning any profit already isn't bad, surely."

Dante seemed to ignore this. He looked troubled, and Hope wanted to ask about David's plans and Dante's own longer-term involvement with the house. However, Natalie had broken the news to her in confidence, and she couldn't betray her friend's trust. Hope hastily opened her notebook.

They discussed what might be needed for the party, then Hope suggested visiting the ballroom to look at where the diners would be seated. Perhaps she could find the opening she needed to ask him of his plans for the future of the house. She already loved working at Moondreams House and desperately wanted to know her new business was safe.

"You go," Dante said. "I'm going out tonight, and I've got things to see to before then."

"Oh?" said Hope. "Anywhere you can recommend?"

"Oh, just a place in town. I haven't been before, but Annie told me about it." He grinned. "She said it was a little pretentious, but I'm looking to impress, so…" He stopped mid-sentence.

"Really? Business, or personal?" Hope blurted before she could stop herself.

"Personal," he replied abruptly. "I'll see you tomorrow, and you can tell me your plans after you've had a closer look at the ballroom and hall."

Hope watched as he stalked away, none the wiser about his future plans for the house and its businesses. She was cross with herself for not asking directly. It was not like her to be reticent when it came to finding out important information.

It was later than usual by the time she had investigated the rooms. She decided to go straight home rather than calling in to see Natalie, as had become her routine. Her friend was opening the door of her car as Hope approached her own.

"Sorry, I can't stop," Natalie said. "Got to dash and sort out my hair. I'm out tonight. It's a bit posh apparently, so I must shower and change." She flung her bag across to the passenger footwell and clambered into her car. With a grin and a wave, she drove away.

When Hope arrived home, she was surprised to hear voices in the sitting room. Usually, her parents were in the kitchen at this time of day.

"Is that you, Hope?" Dot called. "We're in here. Come and say hello."

Hope pushed the door open and peered around. Sitting comfortably, her mum and dad beamed at her. Seated on the opposite side of the room was a dark-haired man.

"Colin?" she gasped. Heat rose up her neck.

"That's me," he said. "We haven't seen each other for … well, ages."

Hope stopped herself glaring at her mother. "What on earth brings you here?"

"Isn't it marvellous to meet again, after so long?" Dot gushed.

"You're not normally this late, love," her dad said. "Busy day?"

"Yes, a major project is coming up."

"That sounds interesting," Colin said. "I, um, called round to ask if we might go out somewhere. I heard you were back." He looked embarrassed and then said, "Just a friendly invitation. I don't know many people, and I know you've been away and all that."

Hope took a deep breath. "When were you thinking?"

"I wondered about popping out somewhere this evening. Unless, of course, you're busy. Washing your hair or something." He laughed a little too loudly.

Hope's thoughts flashed back to their schooldays, when she had considered him brash and arrogant. Perhaps life had bruised him, because now he seemed less confident. Then she remembered that Natalie and Dante were both going out tonight.

Why shouldn't I have a bit of fun? she thought. *Everyone keeps saying I should.*

"I'll have to shower and change," she said.

"Of course. I'll come back later."

An hour later the doorbell rang and Colin stood there, looking smart and handsome. His dark hair was neat and his smile was pleasant.

As Hope descended the two steps from the front door, Colin leapt forwards and took her elbow.

"I'm fine," she said hastily.

"I don't mean to be forward, but I don't want to see you fall."

"Thank you. I've learned to manage."

"Of course. I mean, I know from what your mum's told mine that you're doing really well."

Hope wasn't sure if he was being patronising. She glanced sideways and thought she had better reserve judgement rather than jump to conclusions.

In the car, neither mentioned Hope's injury, but it still seemed to haunt their conversation as they talked inconsequentially. She decided to get it out of the way. "I enjoyed my time in the army, and if I hadn't been injured, I'd be there still." She tapped her knee. "But I was, so I'm making a fresh start and enjoying the challenge."

"I can't imagine what you've had to endure," Colin said, blowing out his cheeks. "Honestly, you are amazing."

"No, I'm not. I've been sharp with people who didn't deserve it, and at times I've been self-pitying, but I'm moving forwards at last."

"All the same…"

"So, do you see anyone else from school?" Hope hastily changed the subject.

After that, their conversation flowed easily and they both began to relax.

"I thought we'd go to the Rosé Glow," said Colin.

"Ooh, upmarket," said Hope with approval.

"A special place for a special event — our shared moving along, that is."

As they pulled up outside the wine bar and Hope gazed up at the pink neon sign, she was surprised to feel a tiny frisson of excitement. This was her first date in many months, and Colin was a pleasant enough companion.

He held open the door for her and then said, "Shall we go to the booths down there, rather than sit here?" The tables by the door were high, with tall stools set around each one. Hope was happy to give those a miss, since it would be tricky to climb onto them. It was considerate of Colin to suggest the booths, she decided.

They ordered their drinks and the waiter brought them over. Hope wasn't sure whether it was the alcohol or Colin's easy company, but she found that they got along well. They had plenty to say and they both laughed at the same things.

Hope was mid-sentence when the door opened and two people entered the wine bar. When she realised who they were, she put down her glass and stared.

Dante had his hand under Natalie's elbow, and she smiled up at him. They looked comfortable and happy together. He leaned down and said something that made her laugh.

"Are you okay?" Colin's forehead creased.

"Sorry. I'm fine. It's my boss, that's all. He said he was out tonight, but I didn't know it would be here." Hope brushed away the scene she had witnessed. It was nothing to her if they decided to move their relationship forward.

Dante and Natalie took seats at one of the small tables. Hope forced herself not to keep glancing across at them, but it was difficult.

On leaving, Hope knew she would have to pass Natalie and Dante. She took a deep breath, pasted on a smile, and approached the couple. On arriving at their table, she introduced Colin and they all passed a few pleasantries before Hope was able to make her escape with her companion.

In the car, their earlier awkwardness returned.

"No one at work knows of my injury," Hope blurted. "I'd rather keep it that way."

Colin shrugged. "Okay." After a moment, he added, "Though I don't see why. It makes no difference to anything."

Once Colin had dropped her back at home and she was in her bedroom, Hope went over the outing in her mind and tried to work out why the evening had finished on a gloomy note. Was it because she had opened up and told Colin so much about her previous life, including her time in hospital? She'd never shared so much with a comparative stranger. Then she had spoken sharply about not wanting her work colleagues to know of her injury.

Or was it because she had seen Natalie and Dante together. They had looked so happy and relaxed in each other's company.

The heat of embarrassment rose up her face.

It was nothing to her if Dante chose to spend an evening with Natalie. Lord, she had rambled on and Colin had had to sit there and listen. She was still a mess. That was probably the end of that friendship.

CHAPTER 15

Hope was surprised to receive a text from Colin early the next morning. *Last night was fun. Let's do it again soon*, he messaged.

I can't believe you let me ramble on so much, she responded. *Thanks for a great evening. I'll let you bend my ear next time.*

Later that morning, in the sanctuary of her flower barn, Hope arranged a birthday bouquet. The soothing work gave her time to contemplate. She had enjoyed the evening, and Colin had changed since she'd known him at school. There was no harm in going out with him now and again — he was a pleasant companion. The buzzing of her phone interrupted her thoughts.

"I'm so sorry," the voice at the other end said. "I'm not able to collect my bouquet, and I need it for tonight. Is there any chance that you could deliver? I'll pay for that, of course."

Hope answered without thinking it through. "Yes, of course." She wrote down the details and agreed a time, after the shop had closed.

As she finished the call, she remembered all the other things she had to do that evening. She needed to complete the floral arrangement at the house, and then there were the table decorations to replace in Natalie's teashop. She didn't have time to go traipsing to the other side of the city. She sighed.

A deep voice pierced through her reverie. "Anything wrong?" Dante stood in the middle of the room, looking up at the stained-glass window.

"I have to drive miles tonight to deliver an order when the customer was supposed to come and collect it," Hope explained. "I need a driver. Someone with their own van who can be flexible and won't mind a commission at any time."

"Maybe a retired person? Probably wouldn't be too expensive."

"I'd have to pay a mileage allowance."

"Yes, that's the best way. How many times a week would you need someone?"

"Two or three at the moment. It'll build up — hopefully."

"Yes, but if you told clients deliveries are only on Mondays, Wednesdays, and Fridays, it would be manageable. Then if you were doing a wedding or something on a Saturday, that would be a slightly different rate for the customer, wouldn't it? You could probably go for it. There would be no net loss."

"That would be such a relief. It's getting to the stage where I'm too busy to work alone but not bringing in enough for an assistant."

"That's normal. We'll look at it when we meet formally next week."

"Right." Hope nodded. "Did you come for anything in particular?"

"I thought I'd buy a gift. Something small." Dante looked around vaguely at the island displays and the shelving across the room.

"Oh! Oh, right." Hope recovered quickly from her astonishment. "Have a wander, or I can advise you."

"I'll take a look. You get on, I can see you're busy." He nodded at the paring knife Hope had inadvertently brought with her.

"My goodness. I should have left this on the workbench. A customer might have been less than impressed."

Hope was aware of every tiny sound as she returned to her flower display. She glanced at Dante as he stood with his hands on his hips, looking at the goods on display. One hand came to the back of his neck and she heard him exhale.

Hope hesitated. "There are some luxury candles in jars over here," she said eventually, moving towards them. "This one isn't overpowering." She took the lid from the glass pot and offered it for him to smell.

"That's a possibility. Do women like this kind of thing? She might have one already."

A woman. Okay, Hope thought. "Anyone I know?"

"Natalie," he answered and looked away.

"Right, oh, well then…" Hope paused. "You can't have too many candles." She laughed. "I've put four or five around the bath. I can lie there and read for ages." She became flustered, having wondered what images she had created. "Or there are pretty little pin dishes. They're always useful for other things. Or maybe a porcelain mug. They're quite delicate." She realised she was talking too much. "I'll leave you to decide," she said, before backing off and standing beside the till. Fortunately, three ladies came through the door.

Hope smiled at them. "Good morning, may I help you?" she asked. Once she had finished serving them, Dante brought her the candle, which she gift-wrapped for him. "I'm sure that's a wise choice," she said, taking refuge in being the efficient businesswoman.

Finally, Hope got back to her bouquet arrangement and finished it quickly, standing back to survey her handiwork. She wiped down the table in preparation for selecting the best coloured cellophane and ribbons with which to finish it off. She was getting quite adept at managing the pedal bin with her prosthetic foot. As she bent to empty the cuttings and petals into it, she spotted something strange hiding under the rubbish. It looked like a bread bag. That was odd — it definitely hadn't been there when she had thrown away the clippings yesterday. It shouldn't have been in this bin either, since the contents would be emptied onto the compost heap.

At that moment, she heard voices as more customers entered. Retrieving the plastic bag and dropping it into the other bin, she hurried to the till, thinking no more about it.

CHAPTER 16

The engagement party for Natalie's mother, Maggie and her fiancé, Rick, was to be a very grand affair. The flower arrangements would dominate the fireplaces in the hall, where dinner would be served, and in the ballroom, where there would be dancing afterwards. Hope would also arrange table decorations, and Maggie had requested a floral door surround between the two rooms. Ahead of their meeting, Hope had prepared some rough ideas.

"There is something magical about your work," Maggie said as she turned the pages of Hope's sketchpad. "The colours, the form, are so stylish. I don't want anything that looks constrained and wired into weird shapes. The flowers need to be full of life and have a sense of movement."

"I understand completely," Hope said. "I hope to create a sense of wonder using untamed, unmanicured designs. The flowers will speak through their scent, their shape, and their texture. Now, what about colours? Perhaps I might suggest veering towards soft palettes with pops of strong, dark colours?"

"That sounds perfect. It's as if you know exactly what I need. I have absolute faith that you'll create just the right thing for Rick and I to celebrate finding each other."

Hope was under no illusion that this commission would stretch and challenge her, but she was excited to start planning the blooms she might use.

Later that day, Hope was due to meet Dante to discuss the hiring of a driver to deliver her arrangements. She waited for him to arrive in her office, eager to show him her designs for Maggie's engagement party.

When he arrived, he studied the sketches. After several minutes, he nodded and said, "I went to an engagement party when I was in France. There was a thing around the door of the church that looked awful. The flowers were dyed such gaudy colours. They could have easily been made of plastic."

Hope looked up at him, wondering if he was about to criticise her work.

"Your designs are so different to those. So many floral arrangements look tight and over-sculpted, but yours look natural and original."

"I'll be using mainly home-produced flowers. It will be calming and restorative."

Dante looked thoughtful and smiled at her. "You have a gift," he said.

Hope blushed at the unexpected compliment. Dante was so handsome when he smiled. His eyes shone and a dimple appeared at the corner of his mouth.

Hope grinned back at him as they shared this moment of understanding. It was almost intimate. She sat back hurriedly on her stool.

Dante cleared his throat. "I've brought you this." He held out a large brown envelope.

Hope frowned as she took it and slid out the papers. She glanced up at Dante, who was avoiding her gaze.

"My father has decided to retire and is handing Moondreams House over to me to run. We've spoken to our solicitor. It won't affect your agreement in any way. All the conditions remain the same."

It was several weeks since Hope had heard the rumours from Natalie, and she'd almost forgotten about them. "What will David be doing? Will he continue to live in the house?"

"He's going travelling in Europe with his companion, Edith. They might settle in France eventually. My father spent a lot of time there when he worked in the antiques business, and he speaks the language fluently."

Hope was determined to find out Dante's own plans. If he was planning to leave or sell up, it could be the end of her dream. She wrapped her arms around her body, feeling a sudden chill of dread. This must be faced just as she had faced many other setbacks in her life. "I thought you didn't really want to be tied to the house and its businesses," Hope said. "I understood that you only came back because your father put pressure on you."

"Yes, well…" Dante took a deep breath. "We've never really got along, my father and I. Yes, I came back because he asked — well, he begged me to. I thought that he was becoming frail or something. I should have guessed it was nothing of the sort and that he wanted something else for himself." There was a silence while he appeared to gather his thoughts. "I'll see how it goes."

"If you have no love for this place, then why stay?" Hope turned from him slightly and played with the paring knife next to her elbow.

"It's not the house I dislike so much, but there are unhappy memories for me here." He stopped and looked away.

"I understand you have a brother," Hope said eventually. "Where is he?"

Dante spoke quietly. "Roy was brilliant at everything. My father certainly thought so. I was always inferior to him. Roy was good at football, the piano, schoolwork, and he was good with people. Everyone loved him. My Auntie Vi, my father's sister, was always praising him. She came to stay when Mama was away."

"What happened to your brother?"

"Roy died when he was just seventeen."

"Oh no. That must have been difficult for all of you," Hope whispered.

"I tried hard all my life but I could never compete with him. Not then and certainly not since he died and became a martyr in Father's eyes."

Hope sat forward. "How did Roy die?"

"He was speeding up the A1, showing off on his friend's powerful motorbike, with no licence and no insurance. They should have been in school. The other lad was luckier. He broke a leg and an arm, but Roy didn't have a helmet."

Hope put her hand to her mouth. The story was sad and shocking. But there was something else. Was Dante experiencing survivors' guilt? Did he perhaps have the idea that everyone wished the brothers' fate had been the other way around?

One minute you were envious of your brother, then cross with him for what happened. And now you feel guilty for being here when he is not.

Hope had been through similar emotions when she'd lost army colleagues, but she'd had help to overcome her experiences.

She realised Dante was speaking again. "I still recall the time Roy took out the girl I fancied while I was away at Senior Scout Camp. He laughed about it, and I lost my rag and hit him." He touched his crooked nose. "He even won that fight, and this is the consequence."

"I'm so sorry," said Hope. "These things run silent and run deep. I know. But we're all here for you — Natalie, Annie, and me."

"Sorry, I'll be fine. I've said far too much. Forget it." Dante rose with haste. "See you later," he said as he marched out.

CHAPTER 17

Setting up for Maggie and Rick's party had been exhausting. Once she had finished placing her flower arrangements, Hope had offered to help Natalie, but it was all under control. She had therefore nipped home and changed into a long, tiered dress in shades of blue that brought out the colour of her eyes, or so Pat had said. The off-the-shoulder style showed off her smooth skin and her short blonde hair shone.

As the meal finished, music coming from the ballroom signalled that it was time for dancing. Most people moved from the hall to small tables set around the edge there.

Hope stood beneath the flowered doorway of the ballroom and watched the happy throng. Among them was Dante, dancing with an older lady whom she recognised as someone from Annie's dance classes. Her heart beat a little faster as she admired his physique, emphasised by his well-cut trousers. He had removed his jacket, and his white shirt complemented his warm skin tone. He guided his partner smoothly, swaying with ease. Watching him, Hope felt a strange sensation stirring inside.

Natalie joined her. "I was so nervous about the meal," she said, "but Ellie and her friends served it all so well. It seemed to go smoothly."

"There were lots of positive comments," Hope added reassuringly. "The starters looked amazing when I saw them earlier in the kitchen, and the desserts were presented so prettily. You're very skilled. Your mum must be extremely proud of you."

"Thank you. There was just a slight hiccup when a lady said she had ordered the chicken dish and was served salmon. I sorted it, though. Fortunately, I had two spares of each dish." She smiled. "I've really enjoyed doing this. I'm thinking of branching out and doing home dining to order. I'd offer evenings and weekends, so if Ellie takes more hours in the teashop, I could fit it in."

"Wasn't one of the problems with Stephen that you both worked too many hours?"

"Yes, but in the long term it would be useful to have a further skill to offer. I might not want or need to be here every day, in the future. I could employ staff to oversee the day-to-day running of the teashop. My training was in catering and silver service."

"So, you'd be more of a manager here, and less hands-on?"

"Yes. That's it."

"You'd be missed, but if it means you could be at home more, then I completely understand."

"Stephen and I have been talking about how we can each reduce our hours."

At that moment, a tall, slim man with a freckled face, grey eyes, and a thick mop of hair approached, smiling at Natalie.

"Speak of the devil," she whispered to Hope. "Stephen, this is Hope. She runs the flower and gift shop in the barn. You've heard me speak of her. She's become a good friend."

They shook hands, and then Stephen addressed Natalie. "I wondered if you'd fancy a dance. It's been a while since we had a lesson together, but I remember enough not to tread on your toes." He grinned at her and winked at Hope. "You've been working extremely hard, Maggie said, when she invited me here."

Hope wondered whether Maggie had been trying to build bridges between Natalie and Stephen. "Go and have some fun," she said. She watched them move away for a waltz, wondering if they would make their relationship work. Part of her also wondered if perhaps Natalie and Dante were not that close after all.

Suddenly, she heard a deep voice next to her and looked round. It was Dante. She watched as his gentle smile became clouded by uncertainty.

"Sorry? I didn't catch what you said," said Hope.

"I asked if you would like to dance."

Hope's heart thumped and her legs felt weak. "No — no, sorry, I can't," she croaked. "I have things to do. I need to check on…"

"It's not just ballroom dancing," said Dante, misunderstanding her panic. "Look. Plenty of people are doing their own thing."

"I can't! Sorry." Hope turned and fled as quickly as she was able. She clutched at the backs of chairs as she crossed the hall, with tears stinging her eyes.

Dante watched Hope leave with a familiar agitation in the pit of his stomach. He thrust his hands into his pockets. Of course she wouldn't want to dance with him. Hadn't he recently told her what a failure he was when he'd spoken of his brother?

He drew himself upright and headed away through the hall. He wanted to go to the barn, his place of refuge, and stand in the peace of its beautiful interior, inhaling the resin smell of the wood, and gazing up at the precious window, but that might be where Hope had fled to. As he passed the enormous flower display in front of the fireplace in the hall, he stopped and plucked a bloom from the side. Nobody would miss it. He held it to his nose and inhaled the scent, which calmed him. He left the hall, deciding to go for a stroll by the lake. Peace and fresh air beckoned as he headed for the door to the kitchen garden.

Dante exited the walled area through the wrought iron gates. As he passed the barn, he glanced across at it and stood for a moment, remembering happier times. Then he frowned. Was that a flickering light he could see through the windows in the roof? The place would burn quickly if there was a fire. As he looked again, it disappeared. He thought that he must have imagined it but decided to investigate anyway.

He tried the door and was surprised to find that it swung open. He poked his head inside and sniffed. There was no smoke and all was dark. He called out, but there was no response. All was safe from damage and if Hope was inside, she obviously didn't want to speak to him. Closing the door softly, he decided that he'd check it was secure before he went to bed. He then wandered across to the flower beds, breathing in their scent before heading towards the weeping willow. As he sat down on the bench beneath its boughs, he closed his eyes.

A sound close by broke in on his thoughts. It was probably a party guest taking a stroll. He stood and parted the fronds, preparing to return to the hall. He wouldn't want to frighten anyone by being here if they had had the same idea as him.

He left the confines of the weeping willow branches and saw a young woman standing near the lake. She had a rucksack hanging from one shoulder — not a guest, then. Gilles closed the gates at night so that cars couldn't drive up to the house, but she could have easily walked in. Perhaps she didn't know that she shouldn't be here at this time.

"Excuse me!" Dante called.

The woman's long, straight hair whipped around her shoulders as she turned her head.

"Can I help you? The house isn't open. We have a party this evening." He took a step towards her and raised his palms to show that he meant no harm. Now he was a little closer, he could see she was probably no older than eighteen or nineteen. "I mean you no harm, but perhaps you should head home. It's getting late."

As he took another step towards her, the woman ran. He soon lost her silhouette against the plants and trees of the parkland.

CHAPTER 18

A few days after the party, Hope met with Dante for their regular financial review. There had been an awkwardness between them since she had fled the dance, which lingered as they sat on opposite sides of the small desk in his cramped office. The meeting was business-like, with none of the easy camaraderie that had built up in recent weeks.

"I'm building the internet flower sales through the website," Hope announced. This had become easier since she had hired Mart, a delivery driver.

"Right. And how is that going?"

"I'm only selling locally at the moment and delivering as far as the city and surrounding villages. It's paying Mart for his time easily."

"How are you marketing that?"

"Clearly that's a key issue," Hope said. "At the moment, it's through social media. I can't compete with the vast sales of the big players. I thought I'd fork out for a big colour spread in the local daily newspaper and the same in the freebie. That's what I wanted to ask you about."

"I think the circulation number for the free paper is about twenty thousand, because it's only weekly. That might be helpful to know."

"I wondered about the cinema. They advertise local businesses," Hope said.

"It costs about five thousand pounds, plus production costs."

"Wow! Maybe not that, then."

"Not yet, but something to consider for the future. It can give you close to eighty thousand views."

"Perhaps you might consider it for Moondreams House?" Hope was optimistic. "All of us could chip in something and do a shared advert. Natalie and Annie might think it would help them in the teashop and the dance school, and you'd get more visitors here. The charge to visit the grounds isn't much, but it must bring in income that's worth boosting."

"I'll consider it," Dante said. "Have you got the current finance report for internet sales? I think we should have a look at that."

Hope opened the folder and passed him her spreadsheet.

"This looks promising," he said. "Definitely worth pursuing advertising in the local papers. Some of the village free posts are excellent value for money, too."

They discussed this aspect of the business for a while longer before Hope moved on. "I was reading an article that said millennials now prefer hands-on experience, so I might start providing classes for small numbers to make their own arrangements."

"Okay, but you don't want to teach yourself out of a job," Dante said.

"But look at the numbers of younger people accessing cookery classes or going to pottery groups. Then they share it on social media. It's absolutely booming, and I need to get in on that. Our marketing must reach the younger demographic, as well as the older generation who have traditionally bought flowers in the past."

As they wound up the meeting, an awkward silence descended.

Hope took a deep breath. "I thought —"

Dante spoke at the same moment. "The house —"

Both stopped abruptly, then Dante tried again.

"I thought the house looked magnificent for the party."

"Yes, it did. Natalie's tables looked sophisticated and elegant."

"Your flowers were..." Dante hesitated, as if looking for the appropriate phrase. "They were very ... skilled," he finished lamely.

"Thank you. I thought the occasion needed to look natural but still grand, and I chose the colours to complement the richness of the chandeliers and curtains in the hall."

"It all worked well."

Hope deftly changed the subject. "When is David leaving for his trip abroad?"

"Very soon," Dante answered. "He'll come and see each of you."

She looked around the tiny space in which they sat. "Will you move into his study?"

"I haven't given it any thought," he said, but Hope doubted that was the case. He didn't seem to do anything without careful consideration.

"Right. I'll be off, then," she said.

As she left the room and made her way back to the barn, there was plenty to think about. Before locking up, she needed to ensure the flowers she had to sell were left in the storeroom rather than the main shop. It was heavy work, lifting the buckets, but it was decidedly cooler through there, and it would prolong the life of the blooms before another delivery arrived in a couple of days. She had learned much about quantities, and now her waste was minimal. She set to her task with determination and was almost finished. She stretched her back and, bending her knee to rest her residual limb inside its casing, she stood for a moment looking down at the final load. The sword-shaped leaves of the gladioli were a perfect contrast to the frills of the red, rich, and vibrant funnel-shaped flowers on their slender scapes. *I do love this work*, she thought. *What could be more invigorating than that colour.*

She was just about to bend and lift the last bucket, when she heard the clack of heeled shoes on the floor. She was going to say the shop was closed, but then she saw who it was and grinned with pleasure.

Maggie came towards her with open arms, and Hope went to return her embrace.

"I had to come and say thank you again, in person. The evening was perfect, and your contribution was simply stunning. So many people complimented you, and dozens took a copy of your leaflet. I think you can expect to be busy for the next few weeks."

"I enjoyed doing it. I can't deny it was a challenge, but I'm so pleased you were happy with it all."

"Happy doesn't begin to describe it. Oh, and look at those gorgeous gladioli. They symbolise strength of character, you know, and also faithfulness."

"I didn't know," Hope said. "I've heard they are the birth flower for August."

"There's much more to the meanings of flowers than that," Maggie said. "It's a fascinating subject — you could make it a strong selling point. Now, in the area of the heart, if these were yellow ones they would symbolise light-heartedness and friendship but red — well, red ones mean passion, desire, and love.

"There's an emotional reaction to receiving flowers, and if you understand the meanings behind those in a bouquet, the attachment is so much greater. Telling people who buy might set you apart from the crowd."

"Maggie, that's an amazing idea. I could have little cards written and included with deliveries." Hope's mind was racing now. "And I could upload examples on my website. Thank you so much."

CHAPTER 19

Hope and Colin went to the cinema two days later. She had found it hard to concentrate on the film. It wasn't a bad movie, but she had found the loud and unexpected noises triggering. Fortunately, Colin hadn't seemed to notice her frightened reaction. She had worked hard to overcome her PTSD, but the sooner she could overcome her fear and trembling, the better.

To calm her nerves, she had occupied her mind with the idea of promoting the meanings of the flowers she used. She had already bought two books on the subject and looked at countless websites. The next morning, she planned to make up small posies, photograph them and upload the images to her website.

As she and Colin walked down the street, Hope's thoughts ran on. With the orders she'd received following Maggie's party, and with drop-in sales at the shop increasing, she was run off her feet.

"Are you all right?" Colin asked.

"I was just thinking about my business. I'm going to have to find someone to help me soon. I'm so busy that it's becoming unworkable."

"You don't want to lose customers because you can't keep up."

"That's exactly it," Hope said. "The finances are difficult, though. It's early days yet."

"Most start-ups go through that stage. You don't want to overdo it, though. It won't be good for business if you look tired and miserable." They walked on a few steps, and then he added, "You could always start wearing more make-up. Distract the customers with a short skirt." He laughed.

"That's sexist, Colin. Would you say that to a male colleague?" Anger bubbled up in Hope's chest. She breathed deeply, trying to relax, as her therapist had taught her.

"Sorry," said Colin. He paused and frowned. "I seem to have said the wrong thing. Let's go to The Bluebell and have a bite of supper."

Hope decided to let it go. She'd expressed her opinion. Colin's remark was outdated and narrow-minded. She'd met people who'd disparaged her when she'd first joined the army, after seeing her small stature. It had got a lot better before she left, especially when others, male and female, had witnessed her determination.

They found a table at The Bluebell and when their food came, Hope ate with enthusiasm, but at the back of her mind was Colin's comment. It reflected how he perceived her, and she wasn't comfortable about it. They'd had several outings, and they had all been easy-going so far. Hope knew him better now. He was usually polite and caring, and much less arrogant than he had been as a youth. They had shared a few kisses, but Hope couldn't see it becoming a long-term relationship, and his comment tonight reinforced that view. Still, it meant she was getting out more, and Dot was happy.

She looked across the table at her companion. He was studying the dessert menu and frowning. A sudden image of Dante crept into her mind. He frowned frequently, and seemed to be unsure of his own worth. A shiver of pleasure passed through her as she pictured him on the dancefloor. His physique in those well-cut trousers… She gasped.

Colin looked up at her. "You're in a funny mood this evening. Do you want anything? I can't decide."

"I'll pass." Hope patted her stomach, wrenching her thoughts away from Dante.

Following a late night with minimal sleep, Hope gathered together all the cards she had been writing until the early hours of the morning. Using cursive script, she had put together short descriptions of the posies she would make. Each one had the names of the flowers and their meanings. She planned to approach Gilles, the gardener, when she arrived at work. Surely he wouldn't mind if she raided his flower beds. She had many of the species she needed in her barn, but a few from elsewhere would certainly help, since the posies were to be small examples of what she could offer. She had separated the emotions represented by different flowers and hues and grouped them accordingly. There was one for passion, deep love, and desire. Varieties of white flowers would represent purity, innocence, trust, and humility. She had planned a posy with yellow flowers for joy and friendship, and another to symbolise good health and strength. During different seasons she would be able to add more, such as poppies for remembrance and sympathy, or daffodils for new beginnings and hope.

With all tiredness washed away, Hope approached Gilles when she arrived at work. He was hoeing between the flowers.

"Hello, Hope. What can I do for you?" he asked. The creases at the sides of his eyes deepened as he smiled.

Hope explained her mission.

"Of course. Not a problem. Which ones do you need? Perhaps I can show you what we have."

They spent a pleasant half an hour wandering between the flower beds, and every so often Gilles would take his secateurs from the leather clip on his belt and snip a couple of blooms for her.

"It makes my heart sing, this sea of petals." Gilles swept his arm out to indicate the flowers that surrounded them. "This place, Moondreams House, is well named. Dreams do come true here."

As Hope headed back to her barn, Gilles's last sentence filled her mind. She entered her domain and took a deep breath, savouring the scent of the wood and moss combined with the flowers' perfume. Perhaps he was correct, and this place was working its magic on her.

As Hope lifted her A-frame noticeboard outside in readiness for opening, she was surprised to see an unfamiliar figure in the distance. A young woman loitered across the grass, leaning against the trunk of a large oak tree. She seemed to be watching Hope. Although the grounds were open to the public, it was unusual for someone to be here so early, and no one was available yet to have taken the woman's entrance fee. Hope was curious rather than uncomfortable and considered approaching, but she had a busy day ahead. She decided she would mention it to Dante the next time they met.

CHAPTER 20

Hope started to assemble her first posy. She'd decided to tie some of them with hessian strips and raffia in a rustic fashion and to arrange others in small trays and vases. She kept an eye on the doorway, although the motion sensor connected to the buzzer would notify her as soon as anyone entered. She looked up when she thought she heard a sound, but there was no one there.

Distracted from her work, she pictured the young woman who had leaned against the tree. She'd had a large bag slung over her shoulder, and her long, tiered skirt had looked unusual on someone so young. She had worn a long, colourful scarf wound around the collar of her trench jacket, and her hair had been long and loose. From that distance, Hope hadn't been able to see her features, but she thought the woman had been watching intensely. As she worked on her arrangements, Hope decided to take another look across the grass to see if she had gone.

She swept the offcuts into the bin, wiped her hands, and lined up her tools neatly on the bench. As she crossed the floor to the external door, Hope remembered the bread bag she had seen a few days before.

The sun was shining on the grass and leaves rustled in the gentle breeze, but there was no sign of the young woman. Hope shrugged and exhaled as she returned to her work, losing herself in the pleasure of her activity. She then photographed her small arrangements, surveying them with pride.

Hope was still distracted when she turned to the door and saw the young woman waiting there. Not having advanced enough to set off the motion sensor, she simply stood in silence.

"Yes? Can I help you?" Hope asked.

She realised she'd sounded sharper than she'd intended; the woman looked like she was about to flee like a startled rabbit. Her eyes were large and brown, and her head jerked around, as if looking for refuge.

"Sorry. You startled me," Hope said quietly. "Don't go. Come in and have a look."

The young woman stepped over the threshold but didn't advance further.

"My name's Hope." She smiled at the newcomer. "What's your name?"

The woman hesitated, then whispered, "Chao-Xing."

"Don't be frightened. Wait here. Don't leave." Hope darted to her back room and returned with a flower. "This is a plant called borage, although it's generally called a starflower, which is much more charming. It's a herb and you can eat it. I picked it in the walled garden." She tossed her head in that direction. "The gardener here, Gilles, helped me to find the flowers that I needed."

"I saw you." Chao-Xing took the flower and put it to her nose. "It smells like cucumber," she said softly.

"You can make an infusion with water, a little wine, lemon, and sugar. It's very refreshing. I've given it to you because its name means courage."

A smile spread across Chao-Xing's face and she laughed gently. "My name means morning star in my father's language, so this is perfect for me."

Hope smiled back. "Where do you live? Are you local?"

"I have to go now. Thank you so much for this." She held up the flower before turning and leaving at speed.

At the end of the day, not having seen Dante, Hope locked her door and hurried to the teashop to tell Natalie about her strange meeting with Chao-Xing.

"What was she like?"

"Very pretty, quiet, and polite. She referred to her 'father's language', so I wondered if she was of mixed Chinese and English parentage."

"What sort of age was she?"

Hope thought about it. "I suppose she was about Ellie's age. What's that? Eighteen?"

"I'll ask Ellie if she knows her. Tell me her name again."

"Chao-Xing. When I asked her if she was local, she fled."

"Strange. Well, as I say, I'll ask Ellie. Now, what can I get you? I might join you, since we're finished for the day. You can tell me how you're getting on with Colin."

"Tea would be great, but no cake. I've had too many meals out recently."

"Ooh! That sounds promising." Natalie grinned.

"And you can tell *me* about you and Stephen. And Dante." Hope tried to make her tone sound casual. "Where are you up to?"

Natalie didn't answer but turned to get the tea. "Hang on," she called from across the empty room.

Once they were seated together with the tea brewing in a pot on the table between them, Hope looked at Natalie with her head on one side, eager to hear whether her friend had been getting closer to Dante.

"It's complicated," Natalie said at last. "Stephen and I are talking. Seriously, at last. We have history and we've shared so much. It's tragic when such closeness falls apart." She paused again. "But I don't want to allow myself to drift back if it's the wrong thing for us."

"I'm guessing that's what your mum would like to happen."

"Yes." Natalie tossed her hair, cleared her throat, and shook off any tears that were in danger of falling. "She invited Stephen to her party the other night."

"I guessed as much. It must have been awkward with Dante there."

"No, not really. I've always been upfront with Dante. We're good friends. So, tell me about you and Colin."

"Colin? Well, he's nice enough, I guess."

"Nice? That doesn't sound exciting."

"I know. I mean, most of the time he's polite and considerate — not as I remember him from school at all. My mum and dad like him, too, and he has a good job."

"Hang on a minute. Your mum and dad aren't going out with him. Don't build a fantasy that isn't there, Hope. You should never settle for second best. If he doesn't set your blood on fire, then don't kid yourself that he's right for you."

Hope didn't answer straight away. She couldn't tell Natalie that Colin knew of her disability yet still accepted her. She wondered if he'd change his mind when he saw it. How would she cope if they took their relationship to the next stage?

CHAPTER 21

Hope didn't sleep well that night. She awoke from bad dreams to a drizzly, dark sky, and her thoughts on her way to work were no more cheerful than they had been the previous evening.

As she entered her shop and lifted the first of the flower buckets to replace it in the showroom, she noticed the wet ring it left on the floor. That was odd. She was sure she had been careful not to slop the water when she had left it there the day before. Then she hefted the A-frame board outside, announcing that she was open for business, and switched on her computer.

There was an email from a customer who had received a bouquet with which she was unhappy. She said that the flowers were not the type she had ordered, although the colours were correct, and the shape of the display did not reflect that on the website. Furthermore, the flowers had lasted for no more than two days before the petals had dropped and the leaves had begun to turn brown. They were for her elderly mother's birthday, and she was highly disappointed.

Hope searched through her folder of orders and invoices but could find no record of the customer. She decided the lady must have made a mistake and ordered from elsewhere. She would respond promptly and suggest that she check from whom she had placed her order.

It played on her mind as customers came. They smiled and made a little cheery conversation, but then they went. This was a lonely place at times. Hope was beginning to realise her whole life was too reclusive, just as her mum had suggested.

Her thoughts turned to Dante, and a surprising warmth spread through her body as she pictured his face with all its moods. She thought of his crooked nose, his eyes when they sparkled with amusement, his hands with their long, sensitive fingers, his broad shoulders, his slim hips, and his deep voice.

Then her thoughts turned to Colin. He was pleasant and kind — most of the time — but she felt no heat. She knew that Natalie was right, but still she wondered whether she should settle for second best, given that nothing was likely to happen with Dante.

Throughout the morning, several customers bought gifts and Hope's mood picked up. She had two orders to fulfil, and she thought about how useful an assistant would be. Perhaps she could eventually offer a floristry apprenticeship.

Partway through the day, Hope looked up to see Chao-Xing standing in the half open doorway. "I didn't hear you," she said, and she smiled as she placed a fresh posy of flowers on the counter. "I'm busy today with bouquet arrangements. I have a driver who'll collect them to deliver later this afternoon, so I need to crack on." She chattered inconsequentially to put Chao-Xing at ease. "The dusting will have to wait." Hope nodded at the feather duster propped in the corner next to the umbrella stand.

"I could do that," Chao-Xing said. "I would be ever so careful."

Hope hesitated. It would be useful, but she didn't know anything about this young woman, and she couldn't afford breakages.

"I won't break anything. You can trust me," Chao-Xing added.

"All right, if you're sure," said Hope, smiling. It would be nice to have some company. "You can put your bag in the back room and hang your coat there, too."

Hope showed Chao-Xing where to start her task. She watched her dusting her displays for a few minutes, before realising that she was taking care.

"I'll be working on the arrangements if you need anything," said Hope, pointing to the array of vases. "When you've done that section, we could have a cup of coffee or tea. Give me a shout when you've finished, or when you've had enough. Since you've volunteered, please don't feel you have to do more than you want."

Half an hour later, Chao-Xing came to watch Hope work. "I really like that," she said, nodding towards the arrangement that Hope had nearly finished. "What are those yellow flowers called?"

"These? They're lisianthus, but they're a species called Corelli yellow. They're unusual because these flowers are usually in shades of pink or white."

"They almost look as if they're glowing with those fringed petals and lime-green buds." Chao-Xing came closer and leaned forward for a better view.

"The lady who has ordered these wants them for her daughter who's just had a baby, but she specified that she didn't want pink for a girl. These flowers signify joy and new life."

There was an expression of wonder on Chao-Xing's face as she gazed at the bouquet. Her enthusiasm both charmed and warmed Hope. While she had been working, she had forgotten the horrid email she had read earlier. Now, with Chao-Xing's praise, her faith in her work was restored. "Shall we have that hot drink? I'm so grateful for the work you've done for me out there."

"Shall I fill the kettle?" Chao-Xing moved towards the corner of the office.

"Yes, do that. I'm nearly finished here. Tea and coffee are in the cupboard above the kettle." When Hope glanced across, Chao-Xing had already found them. "Milk is…"

"Oh, I know," said Chao-Xing absently. Then she gasped and put her hand to her mouth. Colour flooded her face. "I … I … I have to go. I've just remembered, I have to be…" She grabbed her bag and coat and almost ran from the room.

Hope stood still as her eyes followed the retreating figure. How had she known where everything was? Further thoughts occurred to Hope as she remembered the water residues on the floor and the bread bag in the wrong bin. A strange idea began to take shape and she hurried to the door, but there was no sign of Chao-Xing.

CHAPTER 22

From her doorway, Hope spotted Dante gazing across the lake. Since she wasn't busy, she pulled the door closed and approached. She needed to speak to him, but her concerns about Chao-Xing had to wait. Something else wasn't right: she had received an email from another customer complaining about their order. She had to share it with Dante and seek an explanation, because the shoddy product had definitely not come from her.

The grass was still wet from the dismal weather, but the clouds were beginning to part and the temperature was rising. Dante stood tall and straight, with his hands in his trouser pockets. Hope experienced an intense yearning and she paused.

Dante turned at the sound of her approach. He gave a lopsided smile before saying, "I was having a moment of introspection." He cleared his throat and waved a hand. "It's time for me to snap out of it and move on."

Hope's heart gave a jolt. "Move on? You don't mean you're leaving!"

He laughed. It was a loud and spontaneous reaction to her question. She watched his throat as his head went back. "No. I'm afraid I'm staying for now. You'll have to put up with my moods for a while longer. You should have seen your face." He continued to chuckle. "I'm pleased to see I mean so much to you." He looked at her with an expression that she couldn't interpret.

If only you knew, Hope thought, surprising herself. She didn't want him to go anywhere. She would miss their discussions and their occasional sparring. She would miss his twinkling eyes and his mouth with its sensitive lips. She realised with a jolt that Dante had come to mean so much more to her than she had realised.

"Anyway, did you want anything, or are you getting your feet wet for nothing?" Dante looked at Hope's now soaked canvas shoes.

"I wanted to ask your advice. I've had two emails, now, each with a complaint." She explained the situation. "I know I haven't sent out inferior flowers. I've spoken on the telephone to the second customer. We had a FaceTime chat and she showed me what she had received. She's adamant they came from Hope Blooms, but the delivery driver wasn't Mart, and there was no card with the meanings of the flowers attached, which I'm now including regularly. It doesn't stack up. I have no record of these orders."

Dante's usual frown returned to his brow. Hope had an urge to rub her thumb across the lines and ease them away. His words brought her back to reality. "Shall we head back to the barn and look at this further?"

They strode back, and Hope headed for the office and her computer.

Dante followed. "You should take off those wet shoes," he said.

"No! No, it's fine," said Hope hurriedly. "These are the emails. Look."

Dante read and then sat back in the chair Hope had vacated. "Let me see your record of orders and invoices."

"I have checked them. That was the first thing I did." Hope fetched the paper record and then found the online version.

"This is decidedly odd," Dante said. "Have you looked at your website recently?"

"Not since last week."

Dante brought it up, and all looked as it should. "I'll give the website designer a call and see if he has any ideas."

Hope watched his face as he got out his mobile and spoke to Roger, the website designer, explaining the problem.

"I see," Dante said into the phone. "Right. But it's not a common thing? Okay, we'll look into that. Thanks, Roger. Speak soon." He ended the call and turned to Hope. "It seems that sometimes unscrupulous people set up a website with an almost identical name and take all your images and other content. You can and should counteract it, although it's not exactly illegal. They usually choose someone who is making a name for themselves."

"But it's damaging my business, and customers are being ripped off," Hope said.

"Yes. Unsuspecting customers will contact the copycat website, place an order, and pay the asking price, but then they receive cheap alternatives. The scammers pocket the difference, of course."

"That's fraud! Surely it's not legal." Hope was becoming angrier and more panicky. "What can I do? Just when I'm making good headway, this happens." Fighting back tears, she took a deep breath and tried to control her rising agitation.

"I think the first thing is to try and identify the scammer's website," Dante said.

Hope pulled another chair over from the corner and sat next to him.

"Let's put in a search for florists with names similar to this one," Dante suggested. "Roger suggested that the scammers could be using your domain name, with a tiny difference in spelling that might enable it to appear above yours in a search."

After several attempts, Hope suggested, "Try the same name, but spell Hope with an 'a' perhaps."

It wasn't long before the search engine displayed a list of flower and gift shops, and 'Hape Blooms' was near the top of the list. Even though the spelling of the website address was incorrect, it used her header and logo. As they looked at the rest of the copycat website, it had all Hope's images of bouquets and arrangements and the new addition that advertised the meanings of the blooms.

"That's disgusting!" Hope exploded. "How dare they?" She took a calming breath. "What can we do?" Her shoulder rested against Dante's as she leaned forward to better see the screen.

"Let's try to find out how to take down this fake website," suggested Dante.

They settled on sending a 'cease and desist' email to the to the site administrator, requesting they stop the activity. All they could do after that was wait to see if they got a response, before deciding whether to move on to the next step.

Hope also decided to contact the two people who had been taken in by the fake website. She could only hope that they would accept a small flower arrangement from her as a gesture of goodwill, and that they each might use her services in the future.

CHAPTER 23

Hope had thought about cancelling her date with Colin that evening. All she wanted was to keep checking her inbox to see if there was a response to the 'cease and desist' email she'd sent. However, she eventually started getting ready, throwing on a clean top and linen trousers. Her makeup was cursory, and she was just about ready when Colin collected her. They prepared to walk into town, since the weather had turned mild.

"Are you okay with walking that far?" Colin asked with concern.

"Yes, absolutely."

After they had found a table in the pub, he bought the first round of drinks. Once they were settled, Hope smiled and tried to concentrate on the conversation. Her phone buzzed in her pocket, but she resisted the temptation to reach for it.

"So, what do you think?" Colin asked.

Oh, heck! Hope thought. She hadn't been paying attention. She knew Colin had been talking about his career and whether he should accept a promotion. She thought he might have said he'd seen a position elsewhere, but she hadn't heard where. "Sorry, I missed the last bit," she admitted. "It's quite noisy tonight."

"Shall we go? We could have another glass of wine at my flat, or coffee, if you prefer."

"Yes, I'm sorry. It's been a busy day, and I'm not quite with it," said Hope. She slipped on her jacket and he held the door for her as they left. "Tell me the last bit again."

"I was just saying that this new job is about thirty minutes away, but the roads that way aren't too bad. In the short term,

I could even catch the train to Oakham from Peterborough or Stamford. The whole journey would only take about three quarters of an hour if I did that. Maybe in the longer term —" he glanced across at her before continuing — "well ... maybe you might join me. I mean, you could drive to work easily enough, and you would have freedom, away from your parents."

Hope was silent for several moments while she searched for an appropriate answer. Was he asking her to live with him? They hadn't even slept together yet. What was he thinking? No way were they even close to that. "It's hard to say what might happen in the future," she managed.

"Yes, of course." Colin took her hand but said no more, and they walked on in awkward silence until they reached his flat.

Once she was sitting on his small sofa, Hope felt trapped. She refused more wine but agreed to coffee, deciding that coming back to his flat was a mistake. She wasn't in any frame of mind to talk about her future, never mind his.

Colin brought over her coffee. There was no other seat so he sat next to her, their thighs touching. Hope sipped her drink and tried to relax. This was Colin. He was a good friend, and they had laughed together and been easy with each other.

Finally, she finished her drink. "Look at the time. I really better be going. I'll call a taxi. You don't need to come out again."

Colin placed his arm around her waist. "You don't have to leave so quickly. We've been together for quite a while now." He kissed her cheek. "I'd love it if you stayed."

Hope turned to face him and was about to speak when he leaned in and kissed her softly. When he sensed her lack of response, he removed his arm. "Sorry," he said. "Bad timing on my part, I think?"

"Don't be sorry." Hope sat forwards and turned to face him as she perched on the edge of the sofa. "It's me. I'm not in the best of moods. Work has been awful today, and I need to get home to write something up. I'm still a bit of a wreck. I need to get things calmed down." She dug in her pocket and retrieved her phone. "I'll ring for a taxi and see you again soon."

As she sat in the taxi a short while later, she thought of Dante's laughter when they had stood beside the lake. That was the man he was meant to be, she was certain. She wished he wasn't so unsure of himself.

Despite her resolve not to, she couldn't help comparing Colin with Dante. They were similar in height, one sandy-haired, the other dark. Colin was probably better looking, but Dante's crooked nose gave his face character. They both had their insecurities. Colin's arose from his broken marriage, she supposed, but he had been confident at school, and that would no doubt return. She wasn't so sure that that would happen for Dante.

The next morning, Hope dragged herself from her bed after a restless night. Each time she awoke, she relived that moment when Colin had suggested she might move to Oakham with him, and her insides shrank.

"Did you have a nice time last night, love?" Dot asked as Hope poured herself a cup of tea.

"It was okay," she answered.

"You know, you could do worse. Colin's a lovely man, and Heather said he's so much happier these days."

"Mum!" Hope didn't need this kind of pressure.

"I'm only saying, love. You two have a lot in common. Two peas, almost."

Hope took a gulp of tea, threw the rest down the sink, put her mug in the dishwasher and slammed the door shut. "I have to get to work early this morning," she said, feeling like a petulant teenager. Cross with herself, she gave Dot a hug. "Love you, Mum. I shan't be late. I didn't sleep too well last night."

Hope arrived at Moondreams House in good time. Parking her car outside the stable block, she gathered her things and prepared to hurry to her barn. She was eager to switch on her computer and see if the fake website was still active.

As she rounded the corner of the big house, she saw Dante standing at the bottom of the steps. Natalie was descending from the front door. They smiled at each other, and when Natalie reached him, he gave her a kiss on the lips. It was a brief exchange, but it was enough to make Hope hesitate before continuing towards them.

"Good morning!" she called, pasting on a smile. She waved as they both turned towards her.

"We're all early birds this morning," Natalie said.

"Yes, can't stop. Sorry." Hope hurried by. As she strode past, she felt their eyes on her back. Her reaction had bordered on rudeness, and she was filled with remorse. But after witnessing their intimacy, she could not have stood with them. Her emotions were tangled, and she craved the sanctuary of her workroom with its familiar smell of flowers and oakwood.

CHAPTER 24

Dante's heart was beating fast. Hope had hurtled around the corner of the house and must have seen him give Natalie a kiss. As he watched Hope walk away, his thoughts whirled.

While he liked Natalie and they had been friends for ages, they were not in a serious romantic relationship. She had her situation with Stephen to sort out. Dante had been happy to listen to her worries and be supportive, but he was hardly an expert on matters of the heart. She had listened to him, as he talked through his confliction about staying at Moondreams House and he had bought her a candle as a thank you.

As Hope disappeared up the path towards her barn, his thoughts spun on. The only person who had ever really understood him was his mother.

That was unfair. Marie had also been unconditionally supportive until he had driven her away. She had been patient when he prevaricated about moving in together in France and had given him time to come to terms with the commitment. When he had been honest about some of the aspects of his childhood and adolescence, she had listened and counselled with good sense and understanding, allowing him time to become more comfortable with their relationship.

For a while living together seemed to work. They enjoyed the same social activities, liked the same style of living, and laughed together. But then she became persistent in talking about becoming parents and cementing their liaison into something even more permanent. Although he swore to himself he would never be like his own father, he didn't trust himself to take that step.

In the end, she left. He didn't blame her. It was one more failure of his.

His thoughts returned to his mother. She had taken his part and had understood his insecurities. She had always done her best to make him believe in himself and had encouraged him in everything he did. When she had disappeared for those interminable months when he was a child, he'd had no doubt that his father's irascibility had driven her away. Thank goodness she had returned. During the final year of her life, she had encouraged Dante to pursue his dreams, which was why he had left for France after her death. She had died too soon, leaving him with a father who had probably driven her to an early grave.

His anxieties resurfaced when he least expected them to, and this was such a moment. Hope had seen him kiss Natalie, and while it had been little more than a gesture of friendship, he had sensed Hope's embarrassment at having witnessed it.

He knew that he would like Hope to become more than a business associate. Her determination and composure attracted him every time they met. She complemented him with her enthusiasm, bravery and zest for life, and her sparkling eyes and dazzling smile excited him. However, he had little to offer her, other than his business acumen, and she didn't seem to be interested in him as a potential romantic partner.

When Dante turned back to Natalie, she was smiling gently, with her head on one side. "Right, I'd better get on," she said. "Thanks for the drink last night, and for listening to my woes. I'm going to see Stephen at the weekend, and I'll tell him my plans for the business." She nodded towards the teashop. "You've convinced me of the wider business possibilities while keeping the teashop going, and I'm truly grateful."

"Let me know how it goes." Dante gave a brief wave and headed to the flower barn. His soul craved the soft scents of the wood and the flowers. He would make the excuse of asking if there was any response to Hope's 'cease and desist' email.

Flower buckets stood filled with crisp yellow roses; freesias with their rows of small flower buds still tight; lilies on strong stems, their heady perfume emanating from a couple of blooms that were open; and gypsophila with its frothy clouds of tiny flowers waiting to support an arrangement of those more exotic blooms. He breathed in but there was no sign of Hope. She must be in the workroom.

He headed for the room at the back and when he crossed the threshold he saw her sitting with her face in her hands. His chest tightened. Something must be seriously wrong.

Hope had hurried indoors and fled to her desk. Flinging down her bag, she slumped into her chair and turned on her laptop. As she waited for it to start up, she reflected on what she had witnessed. She knew Natalie and Dante had been out together, but to see them actually kissing was too much. Of course he would prefer Natalie to her. Natalie was beautiful and uncomplicated. She had said she was still trying to work things out with Stephen, but clearly that wasn't to be.

Hope went through her emails and found that another complaint had come in overnight. That was all she needed. She read the message twice, and then her hands came up to her face as she fought back the tears.

Dante stood in the doorway. "Hope, whatever is the matter?"

She took a deep breath and dashed a hand across her eyes. Rather than tell him how upset she had been at seeing him kiss

Natalie, she turned the laptop towards him. "Another email. It's similar to the others."

"Ah!" Dante sighed. "We'll need to proceed to the next step." He paused. "But perhaps we should wait another day. I'll give Roger a ring and ask for his advice. Don't worry too much. It's annoying, but together we will get it sorted."

Hope heard the gentle concern in his tone and gave him a small smile. Perhaps Natalie was working her compassionate magic on him and he was becoming more sensitive. Her spirits sank. While she liked Natalie a lot, she couldn't deny that she was envious of her. Hope would have loved to have Dante's arms around her shoulders and to experience the warmth of his lips.

"Are you all right?" His deep voice pierced her daydream.

"What? Oh yes, of course." She retreated into business mode and turned away from him. "The sooner we get this sorted, the better."

"I'll go and phone Roger now."

"Thank you." Hope watched as Dante strode away. The scent of his aftershave lingered and she stood for several minutes, wishing for something that could never be. She then took a deep breath and sat down to research the best way forward. She was losing business, and her company's good name was being sullied. How many other customers had been duped?

She found that it was free to report a suspicious website to the National Cyber Security Unit, and that they acted upon every message they received. She would need to pass on the information to the three disgruntled customers, in case their personal information had been taken and used illegally. They would need to report that to Action Fraud.

Hope couldn't dwell on the problem any longer. She had numerous jobs to fulfil, including six posies and two displays for a client who was organising a large dinner party for a fundraising event. The client wanted something to represent herself and her involvement with the cause, so Hope was planning to use red and pink gladioli to represent strength of character, honesty and moral integrity. The lady had also asked for something to represent gratitude, so Hope had researched and settled on pink hydrangeas. The showy clusters would be a good contrast to the spears of gladioli. The cards that explained the flowers' meanings would have gold edging for such an important occasion.

Hope had no idea how much time had passed as she worked. She'd had to pause her arrangements to serve people who had wanted to buy gifts, and she'd sold an expensive picnic basket as well as a vase and a bunch of iris flowers with particularly unusual colouring. It was frustrating to keep stopping; she would need an assistant soon. After the customers had departed, she hurried back to her arrangements and finished clipping the stems and wiring the flowers. She stood back to admire her work, then turned to fetch the gold-edged cards. There were footsteps behind her.

"What's that?" Dante's voice interrupted her thoughts as he nodded at her cards.

"Oh, hello." Hope watched as he took off his coat and jacket, then folded back his shirt sleeves. Her heart fluttered. "These are the cards that tell the customer what the flowers mean."

"Does that make any difference? If you've made what they asked for, then surely that's enough."

"Sceptical as ever," Hope said. "This client had looked at my website and specifically asked for something that meant generosity, since these are for a big charity event. So yes, it matters. It's giving me an edge among other florists."

"I see." Dante's frown suggested that he didn't. "The flowers look good, though. Anyway, are you in a position to stop?"

Hope's heart skipped at the praise, albeit faint. She put the cards down and came towards him.

"I've spoken at length with Roger," Dante began. "I told him we'd sent a 'cease and desist' email, requesting that the scammers stop the illegal activity, but he said we should get proof of the activity. He'll track down the domain registrar for us. It won't cost much — he'll give us a special rate this first time. He said he's not busy at the moment and to be honest, I think he'll enjoy the detective work."

"So, what sort of proof do I need?"

"Take screenshots of the fraudulent pages and anything that doesn't seem right, like misspellings and the domain name variation compared with your real one. Keep the emails you've received. Roger will check any links to see if they're scam ones."

"I wonder if I could place an order with the scammers. I would keep the full trail of communications and photographs of what I receive. It could be the best evidence."

"I suppose you could. Yes, the more evidence the better. Roger was reassuring; he said that web hosts don't want illegal websites on their platforms, so they'll work with us to take down the site if it's fake."

"Of course it's fake," Hope said sharply.

Dante placed his hands on her shoulders and looked into her eyes. "We'll get this sorted, together. But we will need to be persistent. The web host may refuse to take that site down at first, so we need to collect proof."

His touch was warm. Hope returned his gaze. Standing this close, she could see the flecks of gold in his eyes. She watched his mouth as it curved into a gentle smile. Her yearning for his arms to enfold her was overwhelming. Her knees wobbled as he turned away to look at her cards again.

Dante cleared his throat. "Strength of character? Generosity?" He sounded like he was scoffing. "Really?"

Hope thought he might be hiding his embarrassment at their recent closeness, but she was still annoyed by his sudden coolness. "Yes really!" she said. "It's a good angle."

"I had no idea there were so many meanings attached to flowers." He shrugged. "It seems to be working. Congratulations."

As he turned and exited the shop, Hope felt a mixture of frustration and yearning. How did he always manage to do this to her?

The end of a long day eventually arrived. Hope wanted to collapse into bed, but she had agreed to see Colin and she had to get ready. As she sat on the stool in the shower, and the hot water relaxed her body and mind, her thoughts turned back to Dante. She remembered the warmth of his hands on her shoulders and the look in his eyes. Had she imagined his tenderness? Then she pictured him with Natalie, and resolutely turned her thoughts to Colin.

He was becoming more eager each time they met, and he knew of her injuries, though he hadn't seen them yet. He hadn't witnessed her struggle with PTSD, and he didn't know about the compulsive behaviour, which she had been managing much better recently.

Colin didn't set her blood on fire, but he was kind, and Hope had reached the stage where she craved someone to share her life. Colin could be that person — perhaps.

CHAPTER 25

Hope woke up earlier than usual. Her brain was fizzing; there was so much to do. At five o'clock, she decided to get up and make a cup of tea. If she went into work as soon as possible, she could get on top of the three bouquets that awaited her and restock the shelves. It would be good if Chao-Xing showed up again. She could pay her to do the dusting, since it was a time-consuming task and the young woman was so careful. Last time, she'd even shown an interest in the flowers that Hope had been arranging.

As Hope waited for the kettle to boil, she thought about the first time Chao-Xing had come into the shop. She had seemed nervous and had hurried off when Hope had asked where she lived. Was she in trouble? Perhaps Hope could help. So much had happened since the last time she'd seen Chao-Xing that she had forgotten all about the strange thoughts she'd had about the young woman's sudden flight.

Then, as Hope made her tea, her plans for her upcoming flower arrangements drove all else from her mind. She was looking forward to completing an order for a woman who wanted some flowers for her best friend's engagement. Hope would construct a hoop of moss, which she would wind with gold ribbon and yellow solidago flowerheads, held in place by fine wire. Then, at the top of the hoop, she would affix a large, white daisy. In Norse mythology, this was the flower of love, beauty, and fertility. The hoop would sit vertically on a bed of tiny pink and white rosebuds and eucalyptus leaves, and the whole arrangement would be framed by angel wings constructed from Midollino sticks and wire. The research had been exciting and now Hope couldn't wait to get started.

"You're up early," said Dot, coming into the kitchen and yawning. "I thought I heard you. Is everything all right?"

"Yes, fine. I have a lot to do, is all."

"You need an assistant. Don't you go overdoing it."

"I was going to investigate a grant for an apprentice, but I haven't got round to it. Right, I'm off. Love you." Hope kissed her mum's cheek and hurried to collect her bag from where she had dumped it in the hall the night before.

Only a few short weeks ago the trees across the fields had been stunning in their autumn colours. As she drove, she noticed that they were almost bare of their leaves. There was a fine mist hanging over the fields as she passed, and winter was heralding. It would soon be Christmas, and the season was generating a whole new range of sales. She had ordered decorations and distinctive festive items for her shop, and she had also asked Dante about decorating the rooms and opening the house. He had suggested putting it off until the following year, but she would persevere now she had a better idea of what would be possible. He had spoken of taking plans for the house forwards and there was no way she would allow him to fall into the kind of malaise his father had taken before Annie arrived with her dance school.

As Hope pulled up into her parking spot at Moondreams House, all was silent and dark, and she hastened towards the barn. She saw a dull glow coming from the skylights, which puzzled her. Surely she hadn't left a light on — she was careful about things like that, because she had to make every penny count. She came to an abrupt halt, debating whether to go to the main house for help, but then she managed to calm herself down. Dante would still be in bed; she would feel foolish if she woke him. There had been lights on in the gatehouse where Gilles lived with his wife Angela, but she would look exceedingly absurd if she got them out over nothing.

Summoning up her courage, Hope moved forwards and took her key from her pocket. With her ear pressed to the door, she listened for any sounds from within, but she could hear nothing. She then inserted the key with care, as silently as possible. The well-oiled mechanism turned with only a minor click. She couldn't help taking a deep breath before swinging the door open and sliding inside.

A tuneful humming came to her from behind the closed door of the office. Hope was puzzled. Perhaps it was Natalie or Annie. She edged forwards and the humming stopped. Then she reached out and turned the handle.

Chao-Xing cried out. She was in the process of rolling up a sleeping bag, and as she stumbled back against the wall, she held it against her body for protection. "I'm not stealing. I haven't done any damage," she whispered.

Her eyes darted around, presumably looking for an escape route, but Hope stood in the doorway, and the back door was still bolted. Once again, Hope thought of the empty bread bag and the water droplets on the floor in front of the sink. It all began to fall into place.

Hope put up her hands, her palms facing out. "It's all right. We just need to talk," she said gently. As she advanced into the room, Hope closed the door behind her, and Chao-Xing continued to watch her movements with fear.

"I'm going to make us a cup of tea." Hope glanced at Chao-Xing, who was beginning to cry. She made no move to wipe away her tears, so Hope pulled tissues from a box on her desk and passed them to her. Chao-Xing muttered her thanks and began to relax.

Hope made the tea and indicated that they should both sit. She then went to the cupboard and fetched a packet of biscuits. As time slipped by and they each sipped their tea, Chao-Xing's tears subsided.

"Do you want to tell me what's going on?" Hope asked tentatively. "Maybe I can help." Memories of her time reassuring Afghan women came to the fore as her army training kicked in. She would need to take this slowly so she waited in silence while Chao-Xing gained the confidence to answer.

"I'm so sorry." Chao-Xing hung her head. "I had nowhere to go."

"Where are your parents?"

Chao-Xing paused. "I came originally from Beijing with my father, many years ago. It was a dangerous time. My mother would not leave China. She was meant to join us, but she never has." She took a sip of tea and wiped her nose.

"Where is your father now?" Hope asked.

"He passed away three months ago. The people at the restaurant where he worked paid for all the funeral arrangements. I have no one now." Chao-Xing paused again. Perhaps she was contemplating how much more to share. "I stayed with the restaurant owner and his family for a while, but he has several children. There wasn't enough room, and I couldn't pay him any rent."

"Have you been here since then?"

"I bumped into a girl I know in town. We were at school together. She suggested I stay here … but I've only been here sometimes, to sleep or to wash my hair. I haven't touched anything I shouldn't. Honestly."

Hope was shocked. "What are you eating? Where else do you go?"

"I have food in the restaurant kitchen. I don't need to pay for that. There's always bits left over. Sometimes there are leftovers from the teashop in the big house, too."

"How did you get in here? Have you got a key? I always ensure the door is locked when I leave."

"The girl I know gave me a spare key. Please don't tell. I don't want her to get into trouble. I'm so sorry. I was desperate."

"Is this Ellie, who works with Natalie in the teashop?"

Chao-Xing refused to answer. "I can't say. She was only trying to help me. She is so kind. I didn't want to take advantage. I've looked for a job, but I have no address. I don't know where to go for help." Her tears began to fall again.

Hope wondered what to do. This was a tricky situation. If Ellie was involved, it was serious. Dante should know, but Natalie relied upon her, and dismissal wasn't an option. It would take far too long to get a replacement, and anyway, she fitted in so well. Chao-Xing would need somewhere to stay, and support to find a job. Perhaps a quiet discussion with Natalie would be the best way forward, and together they could decide what to do before involving Dante.

"I must talk to a colleague about all this," Hope said.

"I must go." Chao-Xing leapt up and went to grab her things.

"No, stay!" Hope started to move towards her before standing back. "Please, don't leave. We can help you, but I must talk to someone first." Ideas were beginning to form, but they had to address Ellie's part in it all before they could move forward.

Chao-Xing dropped her belongings again and sank to the floor.

Hope put her arm around her shoulder. "Let us help you. I'll protect you, and you won't be in trouble."

Wide eyes turned to her with fresh tears and, in her silent despair, she nodded.

Hope cornered Natalie as soon as she arrived at the teashop, and they sat at a table together. Hope filled her in on the events of that morning.

"I'll need to talk to Ellie," said Natalie, once she had processed the news. "What she has done is really serious, even if it was for the best possible reason. If something had happened … a fire, or an accident…"

"I know. She clearly didn't think it all through. I'll keep Chao-Xing with me today. I've got a ton of small jobs she can do."

"I'd appreciate it if you were with me when I speak to Ellie," Natalie said.

"That's a good idea. What time does she finish her shift with you?"

"She's here all day, but I think it would be best to wait until after work. I really need her here today. If I speak to her before, she may just leave, and that would be really tricky for me." Natalie frowned and sighed. "What a pickle."

"It is, but you do see why I've had to bring this to you, don't you?"

"Yes, of course. Together we'll decide how to explain it all to Dante. Perhaps he can find a room in the house for Chao-Xing, and she could work with you."

"I've wondered about that too. I need some help in the barn, but I'm not sure if I can afford it yet. I must investigate grants for an apprentice, but it all takes time." Hope looked at her watch. "We'll need to open up soon. I'll see you at closing time. Will you ask Ellie to stay on?"

"Yes. Ellie's a responsible worker in many ways. I'm sure we can sort it out."

"Yes, we will. Together." Natalie gave Hope a hug. "See you later."

CHAPTER 26

Hope had a busy day, with lots of customers as well as orders to put together. There was a flower delivery, too. Chao-Xing was a great help. Although she looked tired and pale, she worked with quiet initiative, managing to chat as she wrapped gifts. She mopped up a carton of drink that a toddler had spilled, reassuring the mother that it was not a problem, and tidied items on the shelves when customers had departed after looking.

Although Hope watched over her, she was free to get on with her flower arrangements. The problem of the fake website was at the back of her mind, but the situation with Chao-Xing was more important, and she needed to decide how to approach the forthcoming conversation with Ellie.

The moment came soon enough. Hope left Chao-Xing with a cup of tea in the office, knowing that she could trust her.

"Please stay here. Don't go running off, and I'll share everything with you when I come back. Try not to worry; we'll work it out." She left her with a warm smile.

On her way to the teashop, she met Dante, who was walking towards the kitchen garden. Hope's heart lurched as she saw his tall frame silhouetted against the setting sun. He smiled as they came face to face. "Hello. I'm on my way to find Gilles," he said. "I'm hoping he has some onions. I'm cooking tonight."

Hope breathed deeply to calm her racing heart. This time it was not from fear. It was something else completely — a feeling that was not altogether unwelcome. "What are you cooking?" she asked.

He chuckled. "A tomato salad in the French style, with seasoned dressing and a baguette to mop it up. It's a lonely affair, and not exactly cooking. Why don't you join me? Unless you have someone else to see, of course."

Images of Colin flitted across her mind. "I … um…"

"Oh, well, never mind. Just a thought."

"Sorry. I must hurry. I need to…"

"Yes, of course. See you soon." With his head down, Dante strode away.

Hope watched him for several seconds. Why had she hesitated? Not coming up with an answer, she headed for the teashop. As she entered, she saw Ellie stacking the used cups and plates onto a tray to take through to the kitchen dishwasher. Natalie was wiping down the counter.

"Do you want a cup of tea?" Natalie asked.

"Let's get straight down to business." Hope nodded towards Ellie's retreating back.

Natalie nodded and called after the young woman. "Ellie, when you've put those in the dishwasher, can I have a quick word before you go?"

"Yes, sure," Ellie answered and headed for the door into the kitchen.

"I'm not looking forward to this," said Natalie. "I can't afford to lose Ellie."

"We'll be gentle with her. She acted with the best of intentions. It's just that she needs to understand the dangers she could have caused."

"Yes, absolutely. I'm not sure Dante needs to know, though. Not when David is about to leave and he seems tense already."

"It would be dreadful if we manage to sort it out and he overturns whatever we decide," said Hope. "The immediate problem is finding somewhere for Chao-Xing to sleep."

At that moment, Ellie returned.

"Shall we sit over there?" Natalie indicated a table.

"Is there a problem?" Ellie's face showed her concern. "I haven't messed up with an order or something, have I? The till balanced yesterday." Her frown deepened when she realised that Hope was joining them.

Hope stretched out a hand and gently touched Ellie's arm. "Ellie, I understand you know Chao-Xing"

Ellie avoided Hope's gaze and nodded, clearing her throat as her cheeks turned pink.

"Then I think you know what this is about."

Ellie flicked a glance at Natalie and then looked at Hope with tears in her eyes. "I didn't mean any harm. Chao-Xing promised me she wouldn't damage anything, and I know she wouldn't take anything. She was in such an awful situation." Ellie stopped talking as tears began to roll down her cheeks. She dashed them away with the back of her hand.

Natalie passed her a tissue.

"Thank you," Ellie whispered. "I'm so sorry. Will I lose my job? Does David know? Will Dante be angry?"

"They don't know at the moment," Natalie said, "but honestly, Ellie, it could have been a dangerous thing to do. If there was a fire, Chao-Xing could have been trapped. I wish you could have spoken to me first."

Fresh tears fell and Ellie gave a loud gulp. Clearly the thought of endangering Chao-Xing and losing Natalie's trust was worse than anything.

"The most pressing thing is to help Chao-Xing find accommodation," said Hope. "I could ask Dante if there is a space in the house somewhere, but then it all might come out."

"He may say I have to go," said Ellie, glancing at the door.

"We have no spare rooms at my mum's and dad's house now that I'm there," Hope said.

"I only have one room," said Natalie. "I could ask Stephen. He has a spare room, but that really wouldn't be ideal."

"I could ask my mum," Ellie said. "My brother is at university now. Perhaps she could use his room for the next few weeks. When he comes home for the holidays, she could share with me. When I offered before, she said she couldn't pay and refused to come. That's why I panicked and took the key to the barn that hangs in the main kitchen so I could have another one cut." A fresh thought occurred to Ellie. "We don't have to tell Mum, do we? She'll be so upset. I've let her down, too."

"I think it's up to you what you say to your mum," Natalie said. "But you should think about explaining it to her in full."

"It's not good to keep secrets from those you love," Hope added. "It usually comes out at some point, and in the wrong way."

Hope and Natalie waited while Ellie telephoned her mum, Ginny. Hope had only met her once or twice, but she remembered her as a warm person who dressed in loud colours. Hope had liked her and imagined she would welcome all waifs and strays with open arms and a cheery smile.

The conversation drew to a close and Ellie nodded meekly at Hope and Natalie. "She said it was fine for Chao-Xing to come and stay. I will tell her what I've done."

When they stood, Natalie gave Ellie a hug. Hope did the same and added, "Let's go and tell Chao-Xing."

CHAPTER 27

Chao-Xing wept tears of relief when they told her about the arrangement. She would go to stay with Ellie and Ginny immediately. Chao-Xing was to return to the barn in the morning, when Hope would talk to her about the possibility of some work.

Hope's emotions were more settled that evening. She was to meet Colin and they were going for a walk in the country park. The paths were level and would present no problem, although it would be dark.

Colin found her in the carpark as she was slipping on a thick coat. "Hi, beautiful," he said, kissing her. "Are you up for this? I thought perhaps we wouldn't go too far. We could go to the Wheatsheaf for a drink afterwards."

"That would be lovely," said Hope.

He took her hand and they set off at a pace that suited her. There was little wind and no frost and so it was a pleasant enough evening with views of the trees and lakes in the ambient light from lamp posts. Most resident birds had huddled down for the night. It was restful.

Colin's fingers were warm as they curled around the back of Hope's hand, but she wasn't comfortable and dropped his at the first opportunity, with the excuse of pulling on her gloves. They chatted, but Hope didn't share what had happened with Chao-Xing. He wouldn't know what to do, unlike Dante. As this thought occurred, she suddenly realised that she trusted Dante enough to share the situation with him. This was a surprise, since she had been planning to keep it between her and Natalie.

Colin glanced across at her. "Is something up?"

"Oh, no." Hope pasted on a smile. "Er … I was thinking of something a customer said. It's nothing. Shall we go for that drink? It's turning quite chilly." She covered her confusion with idle chatter until Colin pushed open the door of the pub and the smell of beer and chips engulfed them.

Somehow, the evening wasn't gelling. Hope realised it was her, and not poor old Colin, who was doing his best to be chatty and interesting. He simply didn't excite her. When they were apart, she never wondered what he was doing or even really thought of him. She couldn't fault his manners, and he was good-looking. Her thoughts drifted to Dante. Their last encounter came to mind, and she remembered the way her heartbeat had raced when he'd invited her to dinner. She could have been sitting with him right now, eating French-style tomato salad. She smiled ruefully at the thought.

Colin frowned. "I can tell you it wasn't funny at the time."

She had been so busy thinking about Dante that she had stopped listening to Colin.

"I'm so sorry. I must have misheard." Hope knew she couldn't string him along anymore; she would need to tell him how she felt. It was awkward, because their mothers were so hopeful about their relationship, and she didn't want to cause a rift in their friendship.

"Hope…?" Colin hesitated. "I wondered if you would come back to mine this evening. We've been seeing each other for a while now. You must know how I feel about you."

Her heart sank. "Oh, Colin." She paused. "I can't tonight. Really, I can't."

"You know I respect you. Look … your disability means nothing to…"

Hope put her hand on his arm. "Colin, I know. It's nothing to do with that. I can't... Look, I didn't want to have this conversation here, of all places. But I can't come back with you. I like you immensely, but ... it's not working for me in that way."

"I see." Colin's chin sank to his chest. When he raised his head, he said, "Please don't say 'we can we still be friends'." There was bitterness in his voice, and Hope knew she was making the right decision, hurtful though it was.

"I'd better go," she said, draining her glass of wine.

"I'll walk you back to the carpark."

"No need. There're plenty of people about, and it's not that far. I'll be fine."

"Of course you will. Army training."

Hope gave a half smile, kissed his cheek, and grabbed her jacket before hurrying to the door.

The journey home wasn't long. Switching off the engine in the driveway, she sat still for several minutes, reflecting. Finishing with someone was never easy, and now she had to tell Dot what had happened. She went inside and got it over with.

Eventually Dot said, "If he's not the right one for you, then that's how it is."

"That's it exactly, Mum. I'm sorry, but second best wouldn't be right for me or for Colin, in the end. I know you're disappointed."

"Darling, I'm not disappointed. Maybe in the situation." She sighed. "But if that's how it is then..." She shrugged in resignation and gave Hope a brief hug.

CHAPTER 28

Hope always arrived at work with time to spare, and Chao-Xing arrived in good time, too. She crept through the door with an air of guilt that Hope was determined to erase. Chao-Xing had done nothing wrong as such; she had just found herself in an impossible position. Chao-Xing had said that her father had passed away recently, but Hope wondered about her mother. She assumed she was still in China, since she hadn't left when Chao-Xing and her father had.

"I can easily find jobs for you here that will keep you occupied," Hope said. "That's if you want to stay and help me? Some of it's mundane, I'm afraid. There are always shelves to tidy and dust, and flowers to be rearranged in the buckets. There's a delivery due today, so if you're up to carrying things in from the lorry, that would be really helpful. If I'm to pay you, I need to investigate grant funding for an apprentice. It may take a little while to apply and organise."

"Oh, I do want to help you here. I love the smell of the flowers, and the things you do with them are beautiful. I'm happy to do anything."

"Until I can pay you a proper wage, I can ensure you have enough food. I'll go and see Ginny to talk to her about you lodging there. I know Ellie has spoken to her mum, but we need to make it a formal arrangement, even though it's only temporary."

"You are so kind. What of David and Dante, though?" Chao-Xing's face became lined with worry. "They may see things differently and report me to the police. I did no damage, honestly."

"I shall have to speak to Dante about the grant application. It may involve some explaining about how you came to be here, because he knows I haven't advertised for an assistant. But don't fret; we'll sort it out."

Chao-Xing dropped her bag and gave Hope a hug. "Thank you. Thank you so much. I will work so hard for you. You will never be sorry to have me here."

When she had disentangled herself, Hope said, "Please, it's all fine. I don't want you to think this is some kind of charity. I need the help, believe me, but I'll only expect you to do whatever any other assistant would do."

With that, they agreed on some regular tasks and had a brief discussion about training that might be possible in the near future.

After lunch, Hope set off towards Dante's office in the big house. The flower beds had become emptier since the onset of the cold weather, but there were still red dogwood stems and winter pansies nodding at the edge. She hoped Dante wouldn't be cross about what she had to say.

The office door was closed, so she knocked. There was no reply, so she pressed her ear to the thick, panelled door. Nothing. Perhaps Natalie would know where he was.

It seemed imperative to share this news concerning Chao-Xing now, when only recently she had determined to shield it from him. Hope realised that she had an urge to see Dante's face. This knowledge had come slowly, but then everything that matters so much, takes time. From being irritated by Dante at times, she found she now craved his presence. Having resolved the situation with Colin, she wanted to move on.

She turned and headed for the teashop, cutting across the ballroom and through the main hall to take the passage to the kitchen. The door between the kitchen and the teashop was open. Hope came to an abrupt stop beside the kitchen door as she spotted Dante and Natalie. They were standing just inside the teashop, out of sight of the customers. He had his arms around her and her head rested on his shoulder. Hope's heart raced as jealousy coursed through her. She knew they were friends, but this was clearly more. And what of Stephen? Natalie had suggested she was coming to an understanding with him. Clearly it hadn't worked out.

Hope took two steps back and leaned against the passage wall, giving herself time to catch her breath and calm down. What a fool she had been to imagine that she and Dante could form a relationship. He had known Natalie for much longer, and their feelings for one another were obviously much deeper than she had realised.

Suddenly aware of her surroundings, Hope rushed to the front door and emerged into the fresh air. She took several deep breaths and gazed across the lawns towards the lake. The willow tree beckoned her. She could take a few minutes to recover before returning to the barn.

As she sat on the bench, hidden by the willow's green fronds, the heat in her chest began to subside. Her head was heavy in her hands, and she leaned her elbows on her thighs for support. After a few minutes, she raised her head.

Deep male laughter drifted across to her hiding place. She stood and parted the long branches of the weeping willow, peeping through towards the house. Dante was coming down the steps, and Natalie waved at him as he descended. Indignation bubbled in Hope's chest. She couldn't decide if it was directed at him, Natalie, or herself.

After deciding it wasn't fair to be cross with either of them, Hope took a deep breath and walked towards the barn. She didn't need to consult Dante about Chao-Xing's situation yet. She was perfectly capable of finding out about apprenticeship grants herself.

She strode through the barn door to find Chao-Xing serving a lady, while another two waited in the queue.

"I'm sorry to keep you waiting," she said with a wide smile.

This was all she needed: her business. She looked across and gave a small nod of approval and reassurance to Chao-Xing before serving the other two customers.

CHAPTER 29

Hope found that Chao-Xing was companionable once she began to relax. She often demonstrated initiative: she re-arranged shelves to display new items, and she made coffee when she saw that Hope was particularly busy. This was a relief since it left Hope free to complete her flower arrangements. If there were no customers and Chao-Xing had completed her early morning tasks, she would come and watch Hope work, occasionally asking questions.

Having done initial research into apprenticeship funding, Hope decided that there was a definite place for Chao-Xing in her business. She decided to speak to David, rather than Dante. She was still chastising herself for hoping that he returned her feelings. So far, she had avoided him, but she'd have to meet with him soon for their regular financial review. They were no longer meeting monthly, since she had successfully completed her probation period, but he still liked to know how her business was progressing.

David was leaving imminently for his tour of Europe with Edith, but perhaps Hope could have one last meeting with him so that she would have something positive to take to her talk with his son. Buoyed with renewed optimism, she approached David's study door and knocked. There was no reply. While she waited, the housekeeper, Mrs M, came through the hall with her feather duster, cloth and polish in hand.

"Hello," she said. "David's working in his rooms this morning." She tossed her chin in the direction of David's apartment up the stairs. "He's asked me to clean in here, since he's off at the weekend.."

"Right. Will it be okay if I go up and knock?"

"Yes, you go on up."

Hope turned to the wide staircase. Brass stair rods held the worn carpet in place, and she carefully made her way up. The wide corridor at the top was dark and large portraits stared down at her from the walls. Arriving at the door to David's apartment, she knocked loudly, unsure how far back it went. Then she heard a distant voice inviting her in. She turned the door handle and peeped around. The room was empty but on hearing footsteps approaching she moved forwards with her head held high. David was walking towards her.

"Good morning, my dear." He wore his habitual white shirt with knitted tie, tweed jacket with elbow patches and corduroy trousers. His only concession to informality was a pair of sheepskin slippers. Hope was reminded of an affectionate old great-uncle. Why Dante had such a bad relationship with him, she could only guess from the little he had told her. Surely that wasn't enough to cause such profound pain between the two men.

"How may I help you? Do take a seat."

Hope launched into her wish to appoint an apprentice and the grant information that she had gathered so far.

"And so you need to finalise that and advertise for someone?"

"Well, as it happens, I have just the person in mind. There is a young woman who has been helping me on a more or less voluntary basis." Without telling him all the details, Hope outlined Chao-Xing's background. "I've had the chance to observe how she works. We get on well, and she's reliable, trustworthy, and intelligent."

"I see," David said, resting his elbows on the arms of his chair and steepling his fingers. "Why have you come to me with this, Hope? Dante needs to be the one involved. I depart with Edith at the weekend."

Hope had her answer ready. "He's exceptionally busy at the moment. I thought you might give me your opinion before I proceed. I will tell him, of course."

A small smile played on David's lips. "Hmm. I see."

Hope got the impression that perhaps he did. Heat flooded her cheeks.

"You will need to speak with him." David put his head on one side, raising his eyebrows. "He thinks a lot of you, my dear. Don't be fooled by his demeanour. It's a cover."

"Right," Hope said uncertainly.

"Your plans seem a good way forward." David nodded. "Make your application if you think it's the right thing to do but talk to Dante. Do that soon, my dear."

"Thank you for your advice," Hope said. "I do hope you have a good journey. What's your first destination?"

"Brussels, on the Eurostar. Then we'll see what takes our fancy. We'll be back in the early spring for a little while."

"Well, have a marvellous adventure."

"Indeed, we shall. We want to leave with no fanfare, as you know. A quiet departure will be best for us … and for Dante. He needs to take all this and move it into the next era." He swept his arm around. "I believe he doesn't know it yet, but he will come to love it more, especially with you … with friends by his side."

Hope hadn't had any recent complaints from clients who had been duped by the false website, and she wondered whether her 'cease and desist' email had worked. The most recent arrangement she'd completed was for a prestigious client, and she hoped it would lead to similar orders. She had hollowed out a watermelon for the pot and arranged flowers to indicate generosity and industry. The globe flowers and gladioli had been great to use because they were long-lasting and showy. The client had also asked for smaller table pieces; for these, Hope had used red clover and bee orchids. She'd sourced these from the Canary Islands, since money seemed to be no object for this client. The meanings of the flowers were written on gold-edged cards, and the end result was sensational, according to those at Moondreams House who saw the arrangements.

Natalie and Hope were in the middle of discussing this when Dante appeared. Hope's heart skipped, but she did her best to quell it.

Dante picked up one of the cards and peered at it. "I can't see it myself," he said, but he shrugged and half smiled.

"Don't be such a grump," Natalie said, nudging his elbow and laughing. Hope turned away and fiddled with a stem.

"I'm not," Dante said. "I'm just saying I don't understand all this 'meanings of flowers' stuff. It's me, I'm sure."

"It must be," Natalie said. "It has certainly caught the imagination of Hope's clients. I mean, just look at these arrangements. They're for a hugely prestigious customer."

Hope turned back with her chin high. "If I get more orders from this customer, I shall be incredibly pleased. My meanings on the cards are beginning to work; they set me apart from the crowd." She turned to Natalie. "It was your mum who gave me the idea."

"But you've taken it forward, and it's paying off," said Natalie.

At that moment, Chao-Xing appeared in the shop, having collected a gladiolus spike from Gilles at Hope's request.

Dante looked at her, but Hope made no introductions and Natalie said nothing.

"I must get on." Hope took the flower.

"Me, too," Natalie said. "Dante, would you like a coffee?" She linked her arm through his and Hope was grateful. She had yet to have the conversation with him with regards to Chao-Xing's position, but she couldn't put it off much longer. Even so, envy coursed through her as she watched her friend leave with the man for who she was falling.

Hope decided to accompany Mart to deliver the prestigious commission. There was no reason to suspect he wouldn't do a good job, but she wanted to make sure it got there safely. They soon arrived at the house, which was on a hill overlooking the country park. The gentleman who lived there was the director of a company, and his wife was the headteacher of a school in Peterborough. The house had an enormous double height window, and a large chandelier was visible between the long curtains.

While Mart opened the back of the van, Hope approached and knocked at the large front door. The woman who answered offered her hand and said, "Good morning. I'm Emma Thorne. Welcome to Thornelea House. You must be Hope Everett. Do come in."

Hope stepped through the porch and cast a glance around at the vaulted ceiling and the long mahogany table. "Are the flowers for this room?"

"Yes, we're expecting business associates for dinner tomorrow. All rather formal, I'm afraid. Between you and I, we need to make a good impression on two of them in particular. They are coming from London." She smiled. "So, I'm anxious to see your flowers."

"I'd better help Mart to bring them in. Where would you like them?"

The lady indicated a large side table covered in a cloth. "If you could place them on there, I will ensure they're carried carefully, after the room is prepared. Then I must get back to school. I'm playing truant for an hour, but I was there until late last night for a governors' meeting."

With the delivery complete, Hope travelled back to her barn with Mart. He was a man of few words, and so Hope was left to her own thoughts. They inevitably drifted back to Dante. She must set up a meeting with him about Chao-Xing. All the information for the grant was in place, and she had only to send it off to the relevant location. She took a large intake of air.

"You all right, there, Hope?" Mart asked. "That were some place weren't it? Fancy living in a place like that. She seemed all right though, the missus, didn't she?"

"I'm fine, thank you." Hope smiled across at Mart. "Yes, Mrs Thorne was lovely. Very easy-going."

She suddenly wondered what it would be like to be mistress of Moondreams House. She would be easy-going, too. Relaxed and confident with the warmth of long history in the house, knowing that she would continue to nurture its preservation and evolution. What plans she would help Dante develop! She turned to look out of the window and her shoulders slumped. An impossible dream.

CHAPTER 30

Hope stuck her head around the doorway into the main shop and called across to Chao-Xing. "I'm meeting Dante later. Before I do, let me show you the final draft of the information I'm going to send."

The young woman came into the office looking anxious.

"Don't worry. I shall be telling him I'm submitting this, but I shan't be adding how you came to be here. I might need to say you're a friend of Ellie's or something and that you have been working here as a volunteer."

"Hope, I can't express how grateful I am and how much I love being here," Chao-Xing said. "Since my father passed away, the owner of the restaurant helped so much, but what you have done for me is beyond anything I could have hoped for."

"You're helping *me*, truly. Now that orders are piling in, I need you here, believe me. Remember we talked about a proper programme of learning and I gave you a document covering knowledge, skills, and behaviours. Did you read the whole thing?"

"Yes, several times." She gave a warm laugh. "I want to learn. If I can help you in here — with arranging, I mean, that would be amazing. Only the simple ones, of course. I could never be good enough to do what you do."

Hope hesitated. Hero-worship had never been her thing. "It'll take some dedication on your part — some studying and even some essays. We will both need to prove this is a proficient area of learning. There will be inspections, I'm certain. They won't give us money for nothing."

"Are you sure you want to do this for me? It'll mean a lot of work for you, too." Chao-Xing's expression became anxious.

"I'm ready to invest in you. I'm sure it will be worth it for us both," said Hope, and Chao-Xing gave her a hug. Hope changed the subject. "We've never spoken of how you came to this country. I know your father had papers, so you're not undocumented."

"Oh no. That must be immensely difficult and frightening for people. Bàba — that's the Chinese word I used for my father — managed to get a Hong Kong Special Administrative Region passport."

"Sorry, I've never heard of that," Hope said.

"Let me tell you the story from the beginning. My dad was such a brave man and his parents showed extreme courage, too. It started with them."

Hope sat down and patted the stool next to her.

Chao-Xing appeared to be thinking for several moments, and then she said, "In the late 1980s, I think it was, the Hong Kong authorities began to employ one worker from mainland China for every person living in Hong Kong. Perhaps that gave my grandparents the idea to go there, and they became uneasy on the mainland. There was always plenty in the newspapers about the situation, apparently."

"It's such a different life there," Hope said.

"They had been waiting for the authorities to grant permission for them to leave for such a long time. Some officials in Guangdong province, on the mainland, took bribes in those days to move people up the list, Bàba told me. It was up to twenty-five thousand Hong Kong dollars for a one-way permit through the authorities. That was a lot of money. I think only a few places were granted each year."

"That must have been so frustrating for them," Hope said.

"Yes, I think it was, especially as the years ticked by."

"Years?"

"Yes, it was years, and then my grandfather heard of some people who would take half the regular fee to smuggle people into Hong Kong." Chao-Xing dropped her chin. "I think perhaps my grandparents took that route. It was never talked about, but that's what I believe, because they managed to get to Hong Kong not long before the handover of the country to China by the British in the late 1990s."

"I know of it, although I don't remember. I was too young," Hope said. "And they managed to stay there?"

"Yes, but they lived in fear. Being sent back, or worse, imprisoned, was a terrible prospect. In the news there was one girl who was only nine years old, and she was taken from her parents whom she had managed to find after being smuggled. The news channels had footage of her in handcuffs. The police found people who didn't speak Cantonese well. That's how they identified them initially."

"So how did your grandparents survive?"

"They learned the correct language of the region while they waited for their permit, and when they arrived they did odd jobs. My grandmother cleaned and did washing. My grandfather mended things. I'm honestly not sure, but eventually my grandfather became legally employed in an engineering factory."

"What about your father? Was he born in Hong Kong?"

"No. He was living with his wife on the mainland."

"So, what happened? How did you and your father get here? Did he go to Hong Kong?"

"Back in the late 1980s, there was a mass sit-in at the Immigration Tower in Wan Chai. Eventually, the authorities passed the Basic Law which gave children of Hong Kong residents automatic right of abode, so my father was able to go legally because his parents were there. My father reached his parents. He got the SAR passport; it's a special one for residents of Hong Kong who also have Chinese citizenship. In time, it allowed him to get a British National Overseas passport. I was born in Hong Kong quite soon after he arrived to be with his parents. My mother was European."

"What did getting the second passport mean?" asked Hope.

"It meant we could come to the UK, but only for six months at first, with an opportunity to apply for limited leave to remain after that. My mother would not come. She was too frightened, I think. She was not married to my father, so he brought me up. We came here together. We didn't need a visa because of the documentation we had, but when we came to England we had so many things to face. It was difficult for my dad to get work, and people were cruel sometimes. We lived in one room when I was very young, but we managed. He worked so hard that I think he wore himself out. His health was not so good."

"What did your father do, for his work?"

"At first he did translation work and studied, and then he got a job at the college. He was fluent in several languages. He did translating in the evenings — technical stuff for businesses. He also worked in the restaurant at the weekends. Then, after five years, he applied to stay here permanently."

"I see. He sounds very courageous and hardworking," Hope said.

"I helped in the restaurant while I was at school, too, before he died. Then you know what happened."

"What had you planned to do after you finished school, before he passed away?"

"I always thought I would go to a university to study languages and business, but my father was ill for quite a while.

I missed a lot of school, because I had to look after him. It was the least I could do."

"Didn't the authorities chase you for missing school or help you out?"

"Yes, but my father was proud. We had food from the restaurant, and I attended school just enough."

"It must have been very difficult."

"Yes. Difficult and sad, to see him slipping away." Tears gathered in the corners of Chao-Xing's eyes.

Hope swallowed and cleared her throat. This young woman had been courageous and resourceful, and now Hope was even more determined to help her.

CHAPTER 31

Hope sat very still as she faced Dante. She had passed him her documentation for the training she would give Chao-Xing. It was a thick pile, and she watched as he turned the pages. It had taken many late nights of researching and typing to get to this stage.

"You've been very thorough. Does this meet all the relevant criteria in each category?"

"Yes, it more than meets it."

"Perhaps we should go through the finances together before you submit it," Dante said.

"I'm not on probation anymore. If I get the grant, I can afford to employ Chao-Xing."

"Why are you showing me, then?"

Hope paused, unsure how to answer. Then she realised that she wanted him to be a part of her decision. "I don't need your approval, but … I would like to have it."

"Go for it," he said. "You have nothing to lose and everything to gain." He flashed her a wide grin, and Hope took a deep breath as her skin tingled. If only he didn't have Natalie in his sights, she could almost believe he was thinking of her as more than just a friend. She wobbled as she stood and grabbed the desk for support.

"Woah! Are you all right?" He shot around the end of the desk to steady her.

The warmth of his fingers under her elbow made her feel flustered, but she straightened her back. She couldn't quite hide her grimace as the end of her residual limb chafed inside the artificial leg sleeve. It had been a little sore for a day or two.

Ordinarily, Hope would have left the prosthetic off and managed with crutches for a few days, but she refused to let anyone at Moondreams House know about her disability. Never mind — she had an appointment with her doctor soon.

"I'll get on and apply for the grant," she said in a business-like voice. "See you later."

When Hope returned to the barn, Chao-Xing was serving an elderly lady in a wheelchair. She was accompanied by a younger woman who looked so like her that she must have been her daughter. The elderly woman was frowning, and the younger one was voicing her displeasure.

"Hope will be here at any moment," Hope heard Chao-Xing say in a conciliatory tone. "I'm sure we can sort this out. Can I get you a tea or a coffee while we wait for her to come back?"

As Hope stepped across the threshold, she looked at Chao-Xing with her eyebrows raised in an unspoken question. She heard the relief in Chao-Xing's voice as she explained that the ladies in question were complaining about inferior goods they had received.

Hope's stomach plummeted, but she managed to keep a straight face as she said, "Please come through to my office. We can definitely sort this out." She led the way to the back room. "May I get you a hot drink?"

"No, thank you. We would like our payment back, and we shan't be recommending you. In fact, we'll be leaving a review that reflects what we received, and it's far inferior to what the photographs on the website promised," the younger woman said. "I wanted something to welcome my mother home following a long and tedious time in hospital. This is what you sent." She thrust her phone in Hope's face.

"I can assure you that is not what I would have sent, had I received your order," Hope said politely but firmly. "I believe a

154

fake website has duped you. We have both been victims of unscrupulous people — let me show you." Hope fetched her iPad.

"Hmph! Perhaps we will have that hot drink after all," the younger woman said, and she told Hope what she and her mother wanted.

Hope stuck her head around the door to the shop. "Chao-Xing, as soon as you have a minute, would you please make us two teas and a coffee? Oh, and all is well with Dante," she added.

Chao-Xing beamed at this news.

"Let me show you this." Hope passed her iPad to the customers.

"Yes, this is what we ordered. It's nothing like the rubbish we received." The younger lady returned the device.

"Now, let me show you this." Hope had split the screen to show the tiny differences between her website and the fake one. "Was your arrangement delivered by a man who introduced himself as Mart and gave you a set of gold-edged cards with the meanings of each flower?"

The older lady frowned. "No," she said.

"I'm afraid you have been deceived, and I have been cheated out of a sale. This has happened before, but I sent a 'cease and desist' email after taking professional advice." She blew out her cheeks. "If you are happy to have your arrangement a little later than you expected, I am happy to make it up for you correctly, and Mart will deliver it to you in the next few days. This will be free of charge, of course."

"I see. Well, in that case… Thank you. That will suffice," the younger woman said grudgingly.

155

"I hope you will revise your assessment of Hope Blooms. I shall be taking further steps to get this fake site taken down for good. It's extremely upsetting for customers and for me, too."

"Yes. Yes, I can see that. I'm sorry if my tone was short, before. I see it's not an error of your making," the younger lady said as she sipped the tea that Chao-Xing had brought.

The older lady looked embarrassed. "With your kind offer, you can do no more for us, and we are extremely grateful for the service we have received today. I realise you are a victim here, too. It's quite unacceptable, and if there is anything we can do or any evidence we can give to support you, we will most certainly do that. When you speak to the authorities, that is."

Hope smiled at them. "Thank you." She saw them to the door. When they were out of earshot, she turned to Chao-Xing and said, "Phew! Crisis averted. I'll send another note to these … these thieves, but I'm not leaving it there, this time."

"Are you all right?" Chao-Xing asked, touching her arm.

"I shall be," Hope said. "Now, my chat with Dante. It went well. I shared with him the programme of training we have discussed, and I'm going to apply for the grant. I believe it will all be fine. I'm so excited to be working with you. I take it all is well with you staying at Ginny's house with Ellie?"

"It's wonderful. I do some ironing and suchlike. I offer to do more, but Ginny won't have it. She says that I'm doing a day's work already and I shouldn't too much when I come back. Sometimes I can take in Chinese food from the restaurant. Everyone is being so very kind. I cannot thank you enough, Hope."

"Nonsense." Hope became business-like. "We must start as we mean to go on and set up a proper programme to cover all the aspects in the training document. We can't be slapdash about it if we're to cover it all. We have two years and a timetable to arrange. Perhaps we can meet after work and sort it out, one day this week. I need to stay on and make the arrangement for those two ladies tonight, but maybe tomorrow or the next day?"

Chao-Xing agreed and gave Hope a hug.

CHAPTER 32

As she locked the door and left the barn, Hope pulled her coat close. There was a crisp breeze as Christmas approached, and the moon was surrounded by a cloudy halo. Perhaps a storm was coming. She had completed the flower arrangement for the two disgruntled ladies, and it was ready for Mart to deliver in the morning. Natalie was long gone, and there were no dance classes this evening. The wind blew leaves around in eddying circles against the walls of the ancient house. Heavy curtains drawn inside the rooms of the house against the night meant the only light was from inadequate bulbs that shone down on the path and all was lonely and dark.

With her head down, Hope limped towards the staff carpark in the courtyard outside the stable block. She'd been standing for too long on a residual limb that was already sore. She was aware that she should remove her prosthetic for a few days, but she had so much to do, and there weren't enough hours for her to be slowed down by crutches. She couldn't have managed without Chao-Xing.

As Hope reached her car, she sank into the seat with a groan. At that moment, Dante emerged from the kitchen to cross the courtyard. Seeing her car door still open, he approached. "You're late tonight."

Hope explained about the resumption of the fake website and the encounter with the two duped clients. "I've been making up the proper arrangement for Mart to take to them tomorrow."

"Do you need my assistance, to deal with the copycat website, I mean?"

She was tired, in pain and out of sorts, and so she answered more sharply than she should have. "No. Thank you. I can cope."

"I only meant…"

"Sorry. I'm tired. I…"

"Goodnight, then." Dante turned and strode towards the stable block.

Hope watched him go with regret, then got into her car. They seemed to be constantly misunderstanding each other.

She had been gathering evidence since the last time the fake website had affected her business, and Mart was going to collect the latest victims' statement in the morning. One strategy, she had read, was to engage the scammers in an online chat and take screenshots to catch them out. She would also need to keep an eye on her social media accounts to protect her brand from impersonators.

Dante reappeared from the stable, carrying a bottle of wine. He was heading across the courtyard, back to the kitchen. Tired as she was, Hope opened her car door and called to him.

"I'm sorry I was irritable just now," she said.

"You look shattered." Dante raised the bottle of Pinot Grigio. "Let me pour you a drink before you go."

There was nothing Hope would have welcomed more, but she said, "I'm driving."

Dante nodded and his chin dropped.

"But I would welcome a coffee."

Dante smiled. She used the hand rest on the inside of the door to heave herself out, wincing as she did so.

"Are you all right?"

"Yes, I'll be fine," she said as she swung the car door shut and followed him towards the shaft of light streaming through the kitchen window. He ushered her in, and she found herself standing in an old-fashioned room with a high ceiling. There was a warm, spicy aroma. "What is tonight's dinner? It smells delicious. Not tomato salad this time."

"No, but it's another recipe I picked up when I was in France."

"Not cassoulet? Please tell me it's not that." Hope chuckled.

"My cassoulet is totally unlike the tins you get in supermarkets."

Hope grinned. "That's the only type I've had, I confess." She raised her hands in surrender.

"In that case, you have to stay and I'll alter your opinion. It's not simple sausages and beans, you know. My recipe has a twist."

Dante's smile warmed Hope's heart as he pulled out a chair beside the large oak table. She sank down but gasped as her residual limb chafed. Dante didn't hear, as he was filling the kettle and then rummaging in a deep cupboard.

As the table was so large, they sat next to each other, rather than opposite. It seemed easier to talk with less eye contact.

"This is delicious and bears no resemblance to what I've had before," Hope said. "What's the secret ingredient?"

"Obviously, I can't divulge that," Dante answered teasingly. "I'd have to silence you."

Hope blushed and glanced sideways to observe his profile. Her eyes lingered on his strong chin, slightly shadowed at this time of day, the dimple in his cheek, and the hair curling around his ears. Her stomach clenched and she took a gulp of wine. They had agreed the food would soak it up before she needed to drive anywhere.

"Tell me about your mother," Hope said in a quiet voice, thinking that this friendly atmosphere would encourage him to open up.

For a minute Dante said nothing, and she wondered if she had overstepped the mark, but then he began to talk. " She was gentle and kind, and said that whatever I did, she would be proud of me. She used to stroke my hair back from my forehead and tell me how alike we were." He paused. "She was so different from my father. He didn't make a fuss or try to comfort me when she left. He only ever seemed to have time for my younger brother, Roy. I think Mama must have found my father difficult, too."

"Why do you say that?"

He laid his fork down and stared at his food. "I remember a time, when she left us for a while. I think she'd had enough. It was his fault." There was bitterness in his voice. "I turned my back on her when she came to say goodbye. I ran away to hide, but when the car was taking her down the drive, I remember running after it and shouting at her to come back. I wanted her to know I was sorry. It was too late, of course."

Tears stung Hope's eyes. This didn't sound like the act of a doting mother, but perhaps she had needed a break. Maybe she had gone on a holiday, or even into hospital, but it must have been confusing for a small, insecure boy. "She did come back, though, didn't she?"

"Yes, she did, but she left again and I had to cope with my father and his moods. She was away when Roy died in the motorbike accident, and then our Auntie Vi came to stay to support my father. I didn't like her and thought she was never going to leave. Then, when she finally did, she said, 'You'll never do as well as Roy did, but you could at least try. Your father needs that.' Not, 'Your father needs you.' I did try, all the time."

"Did your mother return when Roy died?"

"She was at the funeral, but she didn't move back in with us. She passed away soon after that."

Hope wondered why his mother had stayed away. Perhaps she couldn't bear to be in the house after Roy had died, but what of Dante? He was barely a man by then and must have needed her.

They continued to eat, and the conversation became more general. When Dante stood to take the plates, Hope got up to bring the glasses to the sink. "Aargh!" she cried. She sat down again, unable to hide her pain.

Dante rushed back to her side. "Are you hurt? Perhaps I have something that could help. My dad keeps all kinds of lotions and salves upstairs. Or perhaps you've pulled a muscle?"

Hope paused before she answered. "I'm not sure you would have anything for this." She sighed, took a deep breath, and came to a decision. "I suffered an injury when I was in Afghanistan."

A frown flitted across Dante's face. "We heard on the news of some terrible things that happened to our soldiers and the other side."

Hope marshalled her thoughts before speaking again. "Yes, I lost some good colleagues, and some came back with invisible but terrible damage."

"You mean mental health problems?"

"Yes, and that leads to other things like substance abuse and being unable to form or sustain a proper relationship."

"Have you found relationships impossible?"

Hope paused. "I was in hospital for a long time and then in recovery, so I suppose you could say so. I didn't have a close bond with anyone before I joined up and I haven't since, but I was one of the lucky ones." She shrugged and feigned nonchalance. "I have an artificial limb."

Dante didn't know what to say. He schooled his face to remain impassive, but questions crowded his head. He had to be careful not to scare her away. This was clearly a big moment. "Will you tell me how it happened? I understand if it's too painful to talk about."

"It was a roadside explosive. We were in a so-called Mine-Resistant Ambush Protected vehicle on our way to a small village, but they don't always work. Not an unusual story. Six Americans were killed in a blast-proof truck the month before. I lost colleagues and friends. One sustained injuries far worse than mine. I spent several months in a hospital and then in a recovery facility, learning to walk with crutches. Then I was fitted for a prosthetic and had to learn to walk with that. Oh, and I had counselling, of course." She reached for the half-empty bottle and filled her glass, then drank deeply.

Dante filled his glass, too, but he only took a tiny sip. "Did the counselling help?"

"I suppose so." She laughed, but it sounded forced. "Do you remember when we first met at the party that Jacs organised? Someone dropped a tray as I was leaving the marquee, so I dived for cover. It was a sharp, unexpected noise, you see. Self-preservation kicked in."

Dante's heart skipped. His own problems seemed to pale in comparison. He stood, wineglass in hand, took two steps and then returned. "And now? Do you still have that need to duck and hide?"

"It's not so bad. Sometimes I get a bit morose, but my work in the flower shop is great therapy." She smiled up at him and drank some more. "I'd better ring for a taxi. I've definitely had too much of this now." She raised her glass and drained it. "You don't need to worry about me. I'll be fine. You have your own life and relationships to take forward, and I know things are picking up for you."

Dante heard the tinge of harshness in her voice, and he wondered what she had meant by her final comment.

After she'd called a taxi, Hope turned to face him again. "A car will be here in about fifteen minutes," she said. "I'll get another to bring me in tomorrow morning. I guess it's all right to leave my car in the carpark?"

"Yes, of course. Look, I'll come and collect you in the morning. What time?"

"No need. I can sort it out."

"I know you can, but stop being so bloody independent. I'll come.."

Hope gave in, and they agreed when he would arrive.

Dante sat down next to her again. "So that's why you always wear long skirts or wide-legged trousers."

"Yes."

"Ah! And that's why you refused me a dance and left so hastily when Maggie had her party here all those months ago. It all makes sense now."

There was the sound of a car horn and Dante picked up Hope's coat. She turned away from him as he held it up for her to slip her arms through the sleeves. He touched her shoulders lightly and she turned to face him. "Thank you for dinner," she said, a little too brightly. "It was delicious, and that's an honest opinion."

For a moment Dante leaned towards her, but then he backed away and cleared his throat. "I'll see you in the morning."

As she sat in the back of the cab, Hope's mind went over the evening's events. She decided that it was a relief for Dante to know of her injury and since he had no interest in her romantically, it didn't really matter. If Natalie heard, then so much the better. It would not change her opinion for knowing. Pride was important, but too much could also be harmful, she decided. Perhaps she would be more open from now on, should it arise. Her thoughts briefly settled on the training programme she had devised for Chao-Xing. She was looking forward to getting to grips with all the knowledge, skills, and behaviours that she had planned to impart.

Then her mind flitted once more to Dante. No matter how hard she denied it, he invaded her thoughts.

CHAPTER 33

As Dante lay in bed that night, he thought about his evening with Hope. They had shared a lot with each other. He had told her about the death of his brother and about his mother leaving. For years he had buried his emotions, unable to discuss them with anyone. Certainly not David. It was the reason he had left home, then gone to work in France rather than stay with his father after his mother died.

His time in France had been successful. There, wrapped in the warmth of the French sunshine and far away from the painful memories of Moondreams House, he had slowly buried his sense of inadequacy. But his self-doubt had always been there, simmering under the surface. His relationship with Marie had suffered as a result, and he had not been able to bring himself to reach out for professional help.

Unable to sleep, Dante got up and looked out of the window at the garden below. In the moonlight everything appeared as monochrome as the memories of his childhood. His father had driven his mother away and he'd missed her, as he still did. The ache in his heart was deep.

As it was, Hope had shared her secret, too. Dante had been shocked to hear of the injuries she had suffered whilst in the army. But he had been more impressed by her determined spirit. She was brave and resilient. When she experienced fear, she strove to overcome it. She must have done that many times.

He now knew why Hope had fled when he'd asked her to dance. He wanted to fold her in his arms and protect her, but she was far too competent to need him. Her business was taking off remarkably well. She was forging her own path and daring to think big.

He would love to discuss his ideas regarding the future of Moondreams House with her. There were still outbuildings that could be converted into offices or small businesses. They would be ideal for hosting craft workshops, or perhaps an onsite potter or even a blacksmith who could sell cast-iron items. All the new elements of Moondreams House that his father had instigated so far had proved successful. Unless he looked forwards, he would have no place here.

Slowly, he began to think of the future instead of the past.

Dante returned to bed. Everyone who lived and worked at Moondreams House had a purpose. Perhaps that's what he needed to move forward with his own life. A purpose. He should take a leaf from Hope's book and build something for himself.

CHAPTER 34

The following day, Hope prepared to leave for work while Dot remonstrated with her. "You need to take that leg off and use crutches for a while. It'll never heal if you carry on like this."

"But I won't be able to drive home."

"Yes, you will. That's why you got an automatic, for goodness' sake. Be sensible."

"I can hardly carry buckets of flowers and serve customers if my hands are occupied with crutches." Hope kissed her mum's cheek. "I'll take a break on Sunday and stay around here. Perhaps Chao-Xing will open up on Monday."

"That would be an exceedingly good idea. You've been pushing yourself too hard. It's typical of you. You don't know when to give in. Nothing is worth sacrificing your health for."

At eight o'clock, Dante's car pulled up outside her parents' house. Hope was waiting in the hall, leaning against the wall and taking the weight off her leg. She was exceptionally weary, it had been a long day yesterday. She opened the front door as Dante arrived.

"Are you all right? You look a bit pale. How's the sore spot?" he asked.

"I'm fine. I've just had a lecture from Mum, but I've got loads to do."

"Take my arm. Use me as a prop."

Hope opened her mouth to protest, but Dante cut her off.

"You shouldn't be too proud to accept help. It's not a weakness. You of all people should know that, when you consider all the help you've given to others."

"Okay, okay, I concede," she said. As she linked her arm through his, she couldn't deny a small spasm of joy. He took her bag and they walked to the car. He helped her into the front seat. Once her seatbelt was on, she closed her eyes. Her head was spinning a little.

Dante climbed in beside her and started the engine, then looked across at her as she opened her eyes.

"I'll be fine," Hope said and gave him her most dazzling smile.

They arrived at the barn well before opening time, and Chao-Xing came in shortly after Hope. "I'm so excited about my training programme," she said. "I've started to learn the botanical names for the products and how they're grown. I've found a lot of information online, and I've been taking notes. It gives me something to do in the evenings at Ellie's house. There's a section about how the plants are cut by length and weight. I might need help with that. I know we have two years to cover all thirty areas of knowledge, but some aspects will take longer than others."

Hope, already tired and feeling a little queasy, sat at her work table and managed to smile. "Skills will take longer, but when we've finalised our timetable for learning, it'll all be covered. It's great to see you so enthusiastic. I think the Institute for Apprenticeships and Technical Education will accept the occupation programme I sent them, although they will look at it closely to see if they can recommend it to the Compliance Board. Much of it came from the florists' section of their own website, and I gather approval should be given within eight weeks. They will make the proposal to the funding board about which band we might receive. I've arranged a meeting with someone from the institute to get support for a quality strategy and the end-point assessment. That's not for a few weeks."

"It's all extremely time-consuming for you. I'm so grateful, especially since you're already so busy. I can't believe it's Christmas next week."

"I've needed your help more than ever. This next week may be manic, although I'm thinking the busiest time is over. I imagine it'll be last-minute purchases from the shop." Hope paused. "There's something I need to share with you."

Worry flitted across Chao-Xing's face.

"It's only information about me and my circumstances. No need to be anxious." With that, Hope pulled up her left trouser leg to expose her prosthetic.

"My goodness. Is that a false leg? I had no idea."

"Its proper name is a prosthetic." Hope explained about her injury in Afghanistan. She also said that usually it was fine, but at the moment it hurt like hell and she suspected she had an infection. "I can drive without it, but I can't do flower arranging so easily if I have to use crutches."

"I can help carry things, and you can sit here to work. We'll manage together. You must seek medical help. With everything you are doing for me, I shall do whatever I can," said Chao-Xing.

"Thank you. I've been reluctant to let people know. Silly pride, I suppose."

The sound of someone entering the barn broke up their conversation. Chao-Xing gave Hope a hug before going to see who it was.

"It's only me." Natalie came into Hope's office as Chao-Xing went to look after the shop. "Dante said you weren't feeling too well, so I came to see if there's anything I can do."

"You weren't joking when you said working here was like having an extended family. Do you remember? It was when I came to look around."

"That's right. And it is. We look out for each other. Anyway, how are you?"

"I'm fine, but I possibly have a slight infection in my leg."

Natalie looked puzzled.

"Didn't Dante tell you?"

"Tell me what?"

Hope sighed. "There's something I need to share with you. I've just told Chao-Xing, and Dante knows too. I was sure he'd told you, since you two are so close, practically an item."

"We are certainly not…" Natalie paused as Hope lifted her trouser leg. "Oh! I didn't realise. No reason to know, I suppose. Is it hurting you at the moment?"

"Yes. The doctors warned it could be an issue. The end of my residual limb gets hot inside the sleeve, so infections are always a risk." Hope explained about her injury in Afghanistan and her hospital stay, but she didn't go into detail about her PTSD. Hopefully, her trauma-induced reactions were becoming less frequent.

"I can understand why you didn't say anything about it before. Knowing you, you don't want to be treated differently in any way."

"That's true. I don't need pity."

"Absolutely not, but if you need help, that's a different matter. We're all here to support each other, so if you need to take time out, let me know."

"Thank you, Natalie." Hope blew her a kiss. "Dante said something similar."

"That's probably because he's very supportive. I recently confided in him about my relationship with Stephen. Thanks to Dante's advice, he and I are getting back together. We've talked at length about me working more from home now that the teashop is doing so well. I'll do the baking there, and I'm going to look for an experienced manager too. Stephen's got himself an assistant, too. He's only a young school leaver, but everyone has to start somewhere, and Stephen says he's already a great asset. I can't tell you how happy this makes me. We won't have to work such long hours anymore. It's all coming together. Dante has listened patiently to all my worries. He's a really good friend, and I owe him."

Hope tingled with relief. So, Natalie and Dante were not an item after all. "I'm so pleased for you, Natalie. I always hoped you and Stephen would get together again. When I met him at Maggie's party, he seemed so caring."

Natalie grinned then heaved a sigh. "Anyway, I didn't come to talk about me. Let me know if I can help at all. You've been run off your feet lately, I gather. Dante has been worried about you. "

As Natalie left, Chao-Xing came in and made a cup of tea, which she placed at Hope's elbow. "I'll leave you to work on the arrangements in here," she said as she turned away. "I'll deal with the shop this morning. Call me if you need anything from the flower buckets."

Hope took her tea and hobbled across the room to sit in one of the easy chairs. She put down her cup on the little table next to the intricate miniature arrangement she had placed there yesterday. With her head back and her eyes closed, thoughts of Dante invaded. She remembered his smile and the smell of his aftershave. This obsession would have to stop. Dante wasn't in a relationship with Natalie, but that didn't mean he was attracted to Hope. Shaking the thoughts from her head, she sat up and got on with her work.

The bright spot of the day was the email she received from Google. The browser's content removal tool had been another option she had explored with regard to taking down the fake website. The report she sent about the copied content, the statements from her clients and copies of their emails to Action Fraud, as evidence of foul play, seemed to have had an effect at last. The copycat website had been taken down. Hope breathed a sigh of relief. Roger's advice with regards to brand abuse, phishing, and social media impersonation had also been useful. It had been a steep learning curve, but she would be able to keep on top of it all much more easily in the future.

When she arrived home that evening and removed her prosthetic, Hope realised she had let things go too far. Her leg was red and sore, and now there was a nasty lump that hadn't been there before. She would have to ring her consultant's office the next morning.

She immediately called Ginny's number so she could speak to Chao-Xing. "Would you mind opening up the shop tomorrow? I'm so sorry. I'll get there a soon as I can, but I need to ring the hospital for an appointment about my leg. You know where to get a key from, don't you?"

"Don't worry. I'm sure all will be fine here."

CHAPTER 35

The next morning, Hope rang the direct line at the hospital she had been given before she'd left her last treatment. "I think I need to see Mr Walker," she said. When she had arranged her appointment, she sighed with relief.

It was tempting to stay in bed, but the shop needed her attention. She therefore ignored her queasy stomach and aching head and drove to Moondreams House, then made her way to her barn on crutches.

Everything was calm and in order when she arrived. Chao-Xing was smiling at a customer as she wrapped a pretty pottery mug.

Hope swung herself through the door. "Hello, Mrs Plummer," she said to the customer. "Did you find what you want all right?"

"Your assistant has been marvellous," said Mrs Plummer. "I wanted something for my granddaughter to say well done for passing her music exam, and she suggested the perfect gift." She took in Hope's crutches. "What on earth have you been up to?" she asked.

This was another reason Hope had been reluctant to resort to crutches. Everyone she met would ask the same question. "Oh, nothing much," she said. "A slight injury. It'll all be right in a day or two."

"You take care, lovey."

After Mrs Plummer had left, Hope turned to Chao-Xing. "I shall be late tomorrow, too. I probably won't be in until lunchtime at the earliest. Hospitals are notorious for eating up the hours. I'm so sorry. It's not a good start to your apprenticeship."

"Please don't worry. I will manage. Shall I find Dante and tell him?"

"Tell him what?" a deep voice asked. Dante stepped through the door.

Thrown into confusion, Chao-Xing stuttered, "I … I…"

"I have a hospital appointment in the morning," said Hope. "I shall be late coming in, but Chao-Xing will be perfectly fine on her own for that short while. I'll ensure I've completed all the orders for delivery. We're so close to Christmas now — it'll only be last-minute gifts. That's all right, isn't it?" She turned to Chao-Xing.

"Yes, of course, I'll be fine."

"I think anyone wanting flowers will only ask for bunches, too. I gave a cut-off date for major arrangements, and Mart knows where to deliver them."

"You must call me if you need anything," Dante said to Chao-Xing.

"Yes, sir."

"And don't call me 'sir', for goodness' sake." He laughed and his dimple appeared.

Hope's tummy flipped. "Did you want something?" she asked.

"I came to see how you were, but I gather things are no better." He nodded down towards Hope's leg.

At that moment, a customer came in and Chao-Xing stepped forward to serve. Meanwhile, Hope and Dante drifted towards the office.

"I'm seeing my consultant tomorrow," said Hope. "He said this might happen. It's quite common for people who wear a prosthetic, because the sleeve fits snugly and sometimes it gets over-heated."

"Is anyone going with you?" Dante asked.

"No. I can manage."

"I'm sure you can, but sometimes it's good to have company. I wondered if your mum might be with you."

"No, she has a dental appointment. I'll be fine. The consultant's only going to take a look. He'll probably give me some cream or antibiotics."

"The temperature is supposed to plummet tomorrow and the roads will be icy. Drive carefully."

Hope grinned up at him. "Now you sound like my mother. But thank you. I will take care."

Hope watched Dante walk away. She would have liked him to accompany her to the hospital, but she would never ask. Sighing, she turned to her work.

She was determined to leave all the arrangements in good order, ready for Mart to deliver. There wasn't much to do, so she swept her symptoms aside and sank onto a stool at her workbench to finish the last commission.

The following day the weather deteriorated, as Dante had predicted. Hope knew the drive to the hospital would not be pleasant, but she had to keep her appointment as the pain had not improved.

As she put on her coat in the hallway, there was a knock at the door. She retrieved a crutch and hopped towards it. When she opened the door, there stood Dante, rubbing his hands, with his collar turned up against the dreadful weather.

Hope gaped at him. Eventually, she managed, "What are you doing? It's awful out there. You should be at home." She opened the door wider. "Sorry. Come in, quickly."

"I've come to give you a lift. I didn't like to think of you on your own, and apparently it's the worst storm so far this winter."

Tears of gratitude sprung to Hope's eyes so she turned to reach for her scarf. "Thank you. I would have managed."

"Of course you would. But you don't have to manage on your won," Dante said.

"I thought I heard voices." Dot came through from the kitchen, wiping her hands on a small towel.

"Good morning, Mrs Everett." Dante stuck out his hand and Dot shook it. "I came to give Hope a lift to the hospital."

"I wanted to cancel my dental appointment and go with her, but she was determined to go by herself," said Dot. "I'm pleased you're here, Dante. Sometimes she needs to accept help, but she doesn't listen to us."

"I'll stay around, Mrs Everett, and make sure our lass is all right."

Hope was so tired that she wasn't sure she had heard him correctly.

With Dante by her side, Hope shuffled down the path. He held the car door open and she sank onto the seat, manoeuvring her legs around with a grimace. As she sat and waited for him to hurry around to the driver's side the rain speared the window and roof with a rhythm that matched the throbbing in her leg.

Every bump in the road caused a fresh spear of pain in her residual limb, but she was determined not to cry out.

By the time they arrived at the clinic, Hope had to hold onto Dante as he lowered her onto a chair. He then went to report her arrival. While he was at the desk, Hope's vision began to blur. Small dots of light rose before her eyes, before blackness took over. The last thing she remembered before she passed out was the sensation of falling.

Dante turned to see Hope slump forward. Her chair slid and people gasped as she collapsed to the ground.

"Hope!" he cried.

Two nurses came running. They checked Hope's breathing and pulse, manoeuvred her into the recovery position. He hovered, not wanting to get in the way of the nurses but needing to be close and ensure she was all right.

A blanket appeared, and one of the nurses spread it over Hope while the other turned to him.

"What is the patient's name, please?" she asked.

"Hope Everett," Dante answered blankly.

The nurse seemed to recognise his shock and led him to a seat. As she sat next to him, she asked him various questions and he told her why they were there. "We're going to transfer Hope to a ward, but she'll have to go to A and E first so we can assess which is the best ward for her," she said.

"Can I go too?"

"I suggest you go and get a coffee while we sort out her needs, do the paperwork and transfer her. Then you can go to reception and find out where she is."

Dante hesitated and watched as a porter arrived to transfer Hope onto a trolley.

"All right, Mr…?" The nurse cocked her head to one side.

"Troughton," Dante said.

"Well, Mr Troughton, at the moment Hope won't miss you, and she'll need you when she wakes properly. We'll take care of her. You find a hot drink. There's a café on the ground floor near the main reception."

Dante nodded and took Hope's bag as his mind raced. He would need to contact Hope's parents. And Chao-Xing and Natalie. He wondered about his father, but that could wait. David was currently in Switzerland as far as he knew, and anyway, the staff were now Dante's responsibility. He'd go and serve in the flower shop if necessary, although he couldn't arrange the blooms.

He grew fearful about Hope's condition. Perhaps the medical people were being overcautious. Knowing Hope, she wouldn't want to hang around here for too long. He told himself that she would be home again in a day or two.

CHAPTER 36

Hope slept for days, only regaining consciousness briefly before slipping away again. She finally woke up properly when the consultant was on his rounds.

"Well, Miss Everett," said Dr Walker, "you've missed Christmas and all the fun and games of it here in hospital. You've had a tumour, but don't worry — it was benign. You just left it too long, so it gave us all that nasty seropurulent fluid."

"I've missed Christmas?" asked Hope.

"Indeed. You've given us cause for concern, but it seems the worst is over. You're lucky it didn't develop into something much worse. Septicaemia is highly dangerous. You need to do as you're told from now on, young lady." He wagged his finger but smiled. "I gather you've been working hard. Nothing wrong with that, but heed the warning signs. You were lucky this time. There aren't any complications, but it could easily have gone that way."

Hope nodded meekly. After the consultant moved on to the next patient, she was so tired that she allowed herself to drift off again.

When she next awoke, her bedcovers were all over the place. She must have kicked them aside as she slept. She opened her eyes to see Dante sitting on a chair, watching her. Realising that her amputated leg was not covered by the sheet, she hastily pulled it over.

Dante leaned forward and took her hand in both of his. His expression was tender. "There's nothing to fear," he said. "It's made you who you are: the person I have come to love. I wish you'd told me, that's all."

Hope stared at him in astonishment as Dante continued.

"It's true. I love you. I'm amazed I've had the courage to say it at last, but when I thought I'd lost you, I decided I should stay silent no longer. I don't imagine you could ever feel the same for me, but that's all right. I understand. You're so brave, whereas I…" He shrugged.

"You said you love me," Hope whispered.

Dante eased the hair from her face and stroked her forehead. "I'm sorry, I shouldn't have told you how I feel about you, not here, but I've been so worried."

"Why not here? I've been falling for you for ages, but I didn't believe you would want me as I am."

"What a pair we are." Dante leaned down and kissed her forehead, and as he pulled back, his eyes were full of longing. Hope raised her hand to his cheek, and he leaned in again. His lips were gentle as they brushed hers.

"Well, well! At last," said a voice from across the room.

"David!" cried Hope.

"Father! I thought you weren't returning until the spring," said Dante.

"We were missing you all and thought we'd pop back. I know we've missed Christmas, but travel was tricky during the holiday season. Then Natalie told us what had happened here, so I rushed over to see you." David paused. "I wonder if I might have a word, my boy? I can see you are on the mend, Hope. May I take my boy off for a while? I promise to send him back soon."

Hope smiled and nodded.

Once downstairs, David steered Dante towards the front entrance, across the driveway and into the hospital garden, where benches were placed for patients and visitors.

"What's going on?" Dante demanded. "I need to be upstairs with Hope. Whatever it is, surely it can wait?"

"It's waited too long already, my son. While we've been away, Edith has drummed some sense into me. She says I need to share some things with you. I should have told you the facts a long time ago, and then perhaps we could have got on better."

Dante frowned up at the bare branches of a cherry tree. He sighed. "Fine, but please make it quick."

"I need to tell you about your mother and me." David paused. "I know you have blamed me for her leaving, and then her early passing. You believe I had no time for you and that all my love was for Roy. I am partly to blame for that, because I shut myself off from everyone in the belief that things would work out."

"Yes, you did."

"We were all devastated when Roy died, but he always refused to listen to reason. He paid the highest price and he didn't deserve that. Your mother doted on him. On both of you, of course, but she saw something of herself in Roy, I'm certain. There was a certain arrogance there, I'm afraid. They both believed they could do what they liked without any repercussions."

Dante laced his fingers together and hunched forwards, avoiding eye contact.

"She encouraged his wild behaviour and would heap praise upon him, even when he'd done something wrong. It did him no favours. We rowed about it so many times."

This was news to Dante.

"In the end, we became increasingly distant." David paused and took a deep breath. "Well, my boy, she found someone else and left us all." He pulled a large white handkerchief from his pocket and blew his nose. "The other man was a good friend, or I thought he was. I pretended I didn't know, but it hurt me deeply."

Dante risked a hurried glance at his father, but David was staring up at the sky.

"I admit I withdrew from both of you boys. I shouldn't have done that. Roy was so irresponsible, although he certainly knew how to charm your Auntie Vi. I couldn't manage him. I thought your mother would come back to me. And she did. Until she was diagnosed with the final illness that took her from us. I found it hard to keep going. Roy was gone by then, and you left shortly after. I don't blame you."

Dante had been silent throughout, but his mind was racing. Grief was hard enough as an adult, but was it possible that as a child, he had seen things as he needed them to be? His mother had left them for another man. She had chosen to go. His father wasn't to blame. Perhaps he had raised her onto a pedestal. The realisation that his mother was never meant for marriage was a shock. He looked into his father's eyes. For the first time, he began to realise the pain that David had lived with.

"I thought I was protecting you, my son. Perhaps I should have shared the truth sooner, but it seemed disloyal to your mother, and you were always such an insecure little boy. You shook off my advances when I tried to comfort you, always seeming to think I didn't love you," David said.

Dante spoke for the first time. "I didn't know. I didn't understand."

"And that was my fault." David retrieved his handkerchief from his pocket again. "But now you have the chance to be happy. Hope is strong and capable, but she also has compassion."

"I love her," Dante said simply. "I just believed I wasn't in her league."

"But you are, my boy. Go back and see her. Grab happiness while you can."

CHAPTER 37

Three months later

The ballroom was shimmering as the setting sun reflected off the huge mirror above the fireplace. The light from the chandeliers shone on the people who were gathered to celebrate the new season with all its expectation of vibrant energy, perfumes of blossoms and cut grass, and sounds of birdsong and bees. The colours of the dresses of ladies in velvet, chiffon, organza, taffeta, and georgette, were reflected in the huge Spring flower displays that Hope placed earlier in the magnificent fireplace, and on the tables around the room.

Hope wore a full-length blue silk gown that complemented her hair and matched her eyes. When she had seen herself in the full-length mirror, she had felt beautiful. Dante always told her she was, and now, more importantly, she believed it too.

She raised her hem and looked at the small tattoo on the inside of her ankle. It was unobtrusive but meant a huge amount to her. The small bee rested on the sunflower and the whole image reflected the success of the business she had succeeded in building. But more, much more, the meaning of the flower reflected the life she now enjoyed. She had dedicated love and loyalty from the man she loved with all her heart. She had good health and pride in both her body and her mind. She had fought for that and won the battles.

Hope sat and watched the throng of people. Some were drinking and chatting, while others were twirling and admiring the flowers.

"Good evening to each of you, and thank you for attending Moondreams House Spring Ball," Annie said into a microphone. She had arranged the dancing that was about to begin. "Before we continue to enjoy the rest of the evening, Dante would like to say a few words."

Dante took to the stage, and Hope experienced her usual thrill at the sight of him. She would never tire of it. "Good evening, and thank you for coming," he began.

Hope heard little of the speech that followed. She was too focused on his broad-shouldered physique, which was emphasised by his dashing evening wear. In the last few months, he'd become a changed man — more confident and more able to express his emotions.

As he finished speaking, Natalie and Stephen joined Hope. "You look radiant," said Natalie.

"I could say the same about you." Hope watched as Stephen took her hand. "It's not long now until your big day."

"Two months and six days, but who's counting?" Stephen laughed and raised Natalie's hand to his lips. The diamond ring on her finger sparkled.

Chao-Xing came towards Hope, holding hands with a young man. "I want to introduce Lau to you," she said. Then turning to her friend, she added, "Lau, this is Hope. I owe her so much and the fact that I'm doing so well in my apprenticeship is down to her."

"I needed your help just as much," Hope said. "You held the business together when I was ill and you're well on the way to completing your studies with flying colours. We'll have another party then, to celebrate your success."

Hope's friend Jacs arrived with her partner, Malcolm, and introductions followed. "I shall be so pleased when I can get into a smart dress again," Jacs said, cradling her belly. Malcolm placed his arm around her shoulders.

"When is the baby due?" Hope asked.

"Next month, as long as she's not late."

"Gerbera daisies for her, then, if she arrives in April. They symbolise friendship. If she comes in May, then her flower will be lily of the valley, and they either represent completion or sweet purity. Take your pick. Whichever it is, I'll make a special arrangement to celebrate. I first met Dante at the event you organised, so I owe you." Hope stood to kiss Jacs on the cheek.

"I expect to see you on the dancefloor this time," her friend said. "You managed to duck out of it before."

The music for a quickstep started as Dante arrived at Hope's side and slipped his hand into her own.

The others drifted off to dance or to take their own seats.

After that, Annie announced a waltz. As Hope remembered her previous aversion to dancing, she became determined to show how far she had come. She turned to Dante. "Will you guide me and hold me so that I don't look tipsy?" she asked, nodding towards the dancefloor.

He placed his left arm around her waist and held her close as they swayed slowly around the floor. "I'm so very proud of you," he whispered as his cheek brushed her hair. "I want to share my life with you always."

By the time the interval arrived, Dante had disappeared, and Hope was speaking with their friends. She was surprised when she saw him on the stage again.

"Ladies and gentlemen, there is something important I would like to share with you. Please bear with me as I join Hope for one moment." He replaced the microphone and jumped down towards her. When he reached her side, he took her hand and guided her to the centre of the room. A hush descended.

"Forgive me, Hope," Dante said. "I've wanted to do this for so long." He reached into his pocket and took out a small box. As he took her hand, a small gasp rippled around the room. "I would be complete if you agree to marry me as soon as possible."

With tears in her eyes, Hope nodded. As cheers and clapping reverberated around the ballroom, Dante slipped the ring onto Hope's finger. As they clung to each other, music sounded and they swayed gently. Gradually, others joined in.

Hope had found where she was meant to be.

A NOTE TO THE READER

Dear Reader,

Whilst writing this book I met a gentlemen who suffered an injury similar to that of Hope. I spoke with him several times and he told me of his PTSD, hospital treatment, and long recovery. Now he has a young family and a new career, at which he is very successful. He wishes to remain anonymous but he has been influential in this story, and I would like to extend my thanks to him.

It has taken a long time to write this story, largely due to the pandemic and then long-term family illness, but with the support and amazing editorial input from the team at Sapere Books I am now finally able to say thank you so much for buying this book. I hope you have enjoyed meeting some new characters at Moondreams House as well as catching up with some old friends too.

If you enjoyed reading *Hope Blooms*, then I would be grateful if you could spare the time to leave a brief review on **Amazon** or **Goodreads**. As an author, reviews are hugely important, and I am grateful to each blogger, reviewer, and book group member who champions my books. Thank you.

If you would like to know more about my writing, please visit my website **www.rosrendleauthor.co.uk**. You can also **sign up for my newsletter**, where I often offer free gifts and information about forthcoming books. I'd love to hear from you, my dear reader, and you are able to chat with me via **https://rosarendle.bsky.social**, or on **Facebook** or **Twitter**.

Thank you, again, and I hope we will meet again soon through the pages of one of my books.

Ros Rendle

Sapere Books is an exciting new publisher of brilliant fiction and popular history.

To find out more about our latest releases and our monthly bargain books visit our website: **saperebooks.com**

Printed in Great Britain
by Amazon

30783520R00106